TEMPLE BAR

TEMPLE BAR

BAHAA ABDELMEGID

Translated by
Jonathan Wright

The American University in Cairo Press
Cairo   New York

First published in 2014 by
The American University in Cairo Press
113 Sharia Kasr el Aini, Cairo, Egypt
420 Fifth Avenue, New York, NY 10018
www.aucpress.com

Exclusive distribution outside Egypt and North America by I.B.Tauris & Co Ltd., 6 Salem Road,
London, W2 4BU

Dar el Kutub No. 23354/13
ISBN 978 977 416 660 0
Dar el Kutub Cataloging-in-Publication Data

Abdelmegid, Bahaa
        Temple Bar/ Bahaa Abdelmegid.—Cairo: The American University in Cairo Press, 2014
      p.   cm.
        ISBN: 978 977 416 660 0
        1. English fiction
        823

1 2 3 4 5   18 17 16 15 14

Designed by Nora Rageb

Printed in the United States

To the light that shone in the dark recesses of my soul and
cleansed me — to my wife and my son Yassin

With gratitude to Trinity College Dublin, for inviting me to study
there, and also to Ain Shams University

We will send down to you something new and weighty
Bow down
Humbly and devoutly enter the temple
Throw the incense on the coals
Offer sacrifices and take the bread and holy water
Drink the wine and fear not
You will not be humiliated or become intoxicated
Because celestial love will not harm your mind or your body
It is the soul that it seeks

Moon Rising

Chapter 1

Cairo 2003

The rain began to come down in torrents. Moments earlier he had heard it tapping on the windowpanes. He stood up and lifted the blue curtains his mother had chosen when they left Shubra and moved to this house in Maadi. He opened the window and looked out at the water pelting down on the long street. The drops were so big you could see the neon lights reflected in them. A large truck passed by, shaking the whole house. It frightened him and made him feel that the end was near.

The dark woman who lived in the building opposite was also looking, surrounded by her children who never slept. Her daughter Shorouk, who was dark brown, was always doing terrifying acrobatics on the balcony parapet and every time she did so he expected her to fall onto the hard ground with a sharp childish scream that would ring out far and wide. But this never happened. Shorouk's mother was slim and powerfully built. She might have come from noble African stock but she had ended up as a political refugee, or a fugitive from famine or genocide.

All he thought about was the end, because he did not want to continue. This was not voluntary. Inside he had a pressing desire to torture his own body. The rainfall sent an unusual chill through his limbs, as if the water had tempered the fever in his

3

body, like cold water falling on a hot iron bar that the blacksmith has just hammered.

It felt like he was planting hot coals on various parts of his body, putting them on his mouth and pressing on them with his fingers until he could see smoke rising as his body fluids evaporated and he could smell his flesh turning into carbon dioxide. Why the fires now? Why did he want to do that?

Fire wasn't the only way he wanted to end his life. He also wanted to see his blood spilled on the ground. This feeling came over him whenever he went into the bathroom, with its dazzling white floor that made it look like an operating theater. That would come about by means of a sharp razor blade or a whetted knife, and the cut would be right at the lower part of the neck, close to the artery that is always throbbing, or there on the arteries in the wrists. After that bold act the hot blood would gush out and his body would be set free. His tormented soul would escape and go very far away, and he could relax, and everyone could relax.

But how would he dare do that when he was afraid of everything? All he could do now was contemplate the idea of deliberately putting an end to his life, but the deed itself was always postponed. Only now could he say that he had moved on and had changed so much that the idea of putting an end to it made sense to him, so that this torment, this delusion would go away. They had forced him to live and look at his face in the mirror every morning or every evening. They had forced him to convince himself that he was alive and successful and an ordinary person like those around him. Those people had convinced him that suffering was part of existence, that for some reason it had been born with mankind, that it was an honor for him, to give his life meaning, and that it was the way to make his family's dreams come true. His family put him at the center of the circle and made him the focus of their attention. If their dreams for him came true, that would prove to others that they were a family that had succeeded, through bringing this individual into the world.

At times he wondered how his mother would take the news and what her reaction would be. She might be the first person to come across him, unexpectedly, lying on the floor, drowned in his own blood, as cold as a wet towel, lying next to the white bathtub that she had also chosen, because she loved cleanliness. No doubt she would scream, this woman who had recently turned fifty and whose bones were weakened by diabetes. The disease had struck her after she lost her two sisters and her father in less than a year, as if death were testing her capacity to put up with loneliness or as if fate were sending them a sign to prepare for the arrangements of death.

She would be stunned, because he had been the light of her life. She had built him up, watching over him and taking care of him day and night. His life twinned hers and her story was his story—the one he had recorded on the pages of the notebook that he hid away and that she read when he was fast asleep or out with his few friends.

Chapter 2

Shall My Soul Pass through Old Ireland
Irish Ballad

"Moataz"
27 years old
Bachelor
Acquaintances: Many
Friends: Few

What can I do to escape from these characters that surround me? They accompany me everywhere. Now they are phantoms that pursue me in my waking life and in my sleep. They have become elements in my dreams, the rites of my escape and the content of my words. The characters and the people I met on my journey to this distant land, Ireland: the land of rain. Now they sit with me and talk to me. Their bodies and their spirits are heavy rocks that weigh on my chest. I see them walking down the city streets with me in central Cairo, just as they used to roam the streets and lanes of Dublin and Belfast with me. They sit with me in coffee shops as they used to sit in the pubs and bars of Dublin. In its streets they laugh and chat with me, and sometimes argue. In moments of sadness I summon you all; you come to me with open arms. Your warm smiles pull out the sad weeds entangled with the roots of my soul.

I conjure you up repeatedly and send waves of my soul to you through the air and through the stars in the sky. I say, "Always remember me. Don't let your memories of me die. Don't let them drop to the ground amid all the stresses of life."

Here I am now, alone. But in their company I try to create a life parallel to life there, but I always fail and end up disappointed.

I have always tried to forget this journey as if it never happened. It does not matter how long or short the journey is; the time it takes is not important, is not a criterion here, because a moment in the life of man, they say, can contain eons of events and memories.

In the room with the bright white paint and bed sheets the therapist sat me down and said, "Describe what you see around you. How many of them are there? What do they look like? What have they done to you and what have you done to them?"

When I didn't answer he said, "If you can't speak you can write about them. I know you like to write and you're knowledgeable about literature. So why don't you write? Writing isn't therapy, believe me, but I want to get to know you and find out about these characters. You strike me as a nice, gentle person, and definitely the people you know will be the same."

The doctor was gracious and stocky. Sometimes he would smile.

In the evening the room was dark and I was alone with the phantoms. This time I was afraid. I looked at the moon through the window. It was coming closer. It was about to sink down next to my bed and I thought it would have grabbed me if I hadn't been hanging on to the bedposts. I wept a lot. I sat on the floor calling aloud for my brother Nader, for him to come and take me away and keep the moon off me. But he didn't hear my voice and he didn't come. The nurse came in and gave me some milk mixed with a sedative. I wandered off and the phantoms flew away with the moon, far off in the sky.

Chapter 3

Mr Bloom stood at the corner, his eyes wandering over the multicoloured hoardings . . . Hello. Leah tonight. Mrs Bandmann Palmer. Like to see her again in that. Hamlet she played last night. Male impersonator. Perhaps he was a woman. Why Ophelia committed suicide.

James Joyce, *Ulysses*

A Love Story

I walk along the downtown streets. Magical, bustling Cairo. The city that never sleeps; the city that the moon watches over to keep her company. Talaat Harb Street with its large square; Ghad Party posters demanding the release of Ayman Nour. Next to Groppi's, a group of security men are sitting within sight of armored police trucks. The exhausted heads of policemen look out from the small window openings. On the other side people from the Kefaya movement are demonstrating, holding placards that call for 'change' and carrying pictures of Gamal Mubarak. I look behind me fearfully and sneak toward Mohamed Mahmoud Street. I go into the Grillon restaurant and by chance meet an old friend. We sit down.

"You're back and you're just as you were when you left. You're Moataz and you'll never change. Tell me what you've seen and what you've done. Isn't life wonderful? Ah . . . Paris!"

"I wasn't in Paris," I told him. "I was in Ireland, actually, which is quite different."

"What news of her?" I asked him.

"Who?"

"You don't know? Siham," I said.

"She got married," he said coldly.

"Who to?" I asked.

"Someone unknown. Her usual way with men, as you know."

Stunned, I leave him. I go out along the Grillon passageway. I stand a while outside the Automobile Club building. I walk toward the Arabesque gallery. The Egyptian Museum is in front of me with its bright lights. The Cleopatra Hotel. With Kentucky Fried Chicken on my left, I cross the road to the other side and come to Ramadan's newspaper kiosk. I stand in front of it leafing through the newspapers and magazines. I'm hoping to find *Masrah* magazine, which covers theater. I'd like to see Siham by chance. I won't go out of my way to see her. I just evoke her in my memory. She comes to me, maybe burdened with a sense that she's neglected me, or perhaps she's pretending, or perhaps she loves me and is avoiding me, as I sometimes do with other women.

Suddenly I found her standing in front of me, as beautiful and radiant as Isis. Her old magic hadn't dimmed. In fact she was more beautiful than ever. I smell her perfume and it makes my head spin.

She was wearing a dark blue coat and a red hat the color of boiling blood when I heard the news that she had married again. She was holding her son in her arms and she said, "Say hello to Uncle Moataz."

"Uncle Moataz who sends us flowers," said the boy without hesitation.

There was her husband too, bald and swarthy with sharp features. We said hello and shook hands. In a dramatic tone of voice, I said how delighted I was that they were married and how I wished them every happiness.

When he saw me he moved closer to her like a shepherd when one of his sheep has strayed and he goes after it to protect it from danger. You understood that well. You stuck to him and held his hand, as you usually do with the men you love. You looked into my eyes as though you wanted to tell me that you were happy and that you weren't alone. But I think this was deliberate, conscious acting on your part, of the kind you're used to on the stage. You were playing the role of the obedient and loving wife for all covetous, envious men and former lovers to see, and sending the message that others, men and women, should rejoice because those in love should always hope that the ones they love will be happy, even with someone else. But what you were doing was far from honest, when you looked into my eyes, after all the years I've loved you. You took your young son's hand in one hand and your husband by the other hand. Then you left and I stayed where I was, with a sense of foreboding, savoring the smell of you.

I will continue to write about you with all the countless words of love, and I shall always remain the admirer whose existence you never referred to in your stories or in real life.

You will always remain the existential project for the sake of which I continue. In moments of inadvertence we converge and our bodies cease to matter. Differences of ideology and class dissolve, reduced to one level—the level of the soul, or love.

You will always remain so. I evoke you whenever I want. And you walk in on me without my leave and you give my life meaning. You shine light into the dark recesses of my soul. That's how I will be, and that's how you will be, meeting each other by chance. And you will always be with the other man and I will always be alone. We won't let each other go beyond their limits. We have mapped out this destiny for ourselves. The fates have firmly sealed our futures. You may not know that I am writing about you. Maybe you don't have time to read me, or even to know me. Maybe you'll accuse me of invading your privacy and harassing you on the pages of this notebook. You'll say, "Why is he making a legend out of me when I'm just an ordinary person?" and maybe you'll feel proud and throw my book on the table in the morning for your husband to read the title of the novel, *Land of Rain*, and the name of the author, and he'll be more interested in reading the book. Maybe he'll look into your eyes to show that he doesn't mind and go out to look for the book in Madbouly or Shorouk bookshops to find you between the lines. Or maybe he'll be stunned when he finds out the truth—that I love you unrequitedly and have done for a long time, and that you neglect me and I cannot get close to you because you're a dangerous woman and because you eat men up as readily as you breathe the air. Or perhaps he'll be pleased because he hadn't been able to identify the unknown lover and he'll tell himself that it was a coincidence that he found the novel on the table in the morning. No doubt he'll come home in the evening to play the man's role with you, trying to play out the fable of virility, aiming to defy all the men he imagined that you desired.

"Will you marry me?"

Before I mouth the words, I know the answer will be no. So I was reluctant to ask you, and maybe the idea never occurred to me.

But I had already offered a token of my love.

Do you remember the gold pendant I gave you as a birthday present, the one in the shape of the letter *seen*, the first letter of your name?

I couldn't sleep for two nights, uncertain what I should buy you. I borrowed the money from my kind sister. She also suggested the idea of a pendant and said it would be best to buy a gold one. I went to several streets in Dokki where there are gold shops, browsing to buy the pendant for you. At the time you may have been dressing up for someone else and indifferent to me. I write about you like this, not to make fun of how you treated me, but because I want to preserve the memory of buying you something that would always be with you—a pendant you would hang on your breast, next to your heart, to eavesdrop on what goes on inside you, to look deep inside you and inform me of your secrets. Do you still have it? Or maybe it disappeared inside you and no longer exists, or perhaps the other man threw it aside in a moment of passion, unable to believe that it had a license to perch on your breasts and explore them.

I was always trying to confess my love for you and my wish to be closer, in my desire to get to know you and to commune with your spirit. At that time you had achievements to your name: you were appearing on the stage and you wrote things that many men were interested in, whereas I was weak and poor. No one was interested in me. So I kept to myself, and my ideas about the relationship between men and women were vague, unclear. I would ask myself, "What should I do to make myself attractive to her? Because I'm not handsome and I have absolutely no experience of love and I'm poor, and before moving to Maadi I was living in a modest home in Shubra that would serve only as the setting for a novel with a miserable hero who is close to madness or suicide." My heart drew me to you and my body kept away from you and didn't understand what you wanted. My tongue was not trained to put together convincing words of praise. You were superior to me in every way, and I was wallowing in hesitation and failure.

I asked my friends for advice, and they said, "You don't suit her and she wouldn't be satisfied with a man like you. You'd do best to join up with us, hang out with us often, and you might learn the basics of manliness, 'toughen up a little,' strengthen your resolve and make yourself able to win her over. Venture into the world of men first. Because Adam was created alone and was self-sufficient. The female came later to add a feminine touch and make him a complete human, and then she discovered his weak spots."

I went along with them. We stayed up late together. We shared the same beds. We wrote prose poems. We read Trotsky, Che's diaries, Hitler's *Mein Kampf*, Sartre's *Nausea*, Mahfouz's *The Harafish*, Khairy Shalaby's *The Lodging House* and al-Ghitani's *The Book of Epiphanies*. We shared our bread and kissed the lips of the same women. But none of this distracted me from my love for you.

But I couldn't approach you. There seemed to be a wall keeping us apart. I was immobile and you were on the move. I was hesitant, while you were determined to fulfill your aspirations.

A friend of mine, who also knows her, told me, "Don't go near her. She'll burn you and you won't be Moataz ever again. You'll just be a bit player in her life, and you'll never be the star." But they didn't know you the way I knew you.

All they can see is that lost look in your eyes, the confidence in your step and your serious tone of voice. But I can feel your warmth; I can feel the tension in your soul and your desire to reach perfection and fulfillment with the ideal man, because you're very shy, very hesitant, very weak, and everything you do is a mask, a theatrical prop.

But in the end I'm convinced that in your life I will keep playing the role of prompter, whose voice the audience can faintly hear, though they will never see him and he will not go up on stage to greet the audience. I was walking past the Takaiba café, weighed down by the regrets of lost years, when I saw another woman sitting to the side, stretching out her fabulous hair, sitting awkwardly on the edge of her chair, and looking at me with eyes that come from the deserts of lost times. I tried to smile and to drive the specter of the first woman out of my life. I later found out that her name was Hanan and she was studying archeology. I joked with her and said, "By meeting me you've discovered a whole pharaonic family with plenty of treasures and mummies." "You're a big treasure," she said.

Hanan was going on digs with foreign missions in the oases and in Dahshour. We often met at the Egyptian Museum, where Zahi Hawass and Ali Radwan gave their lectures about Egyptian antiquities. She was a hard-working student who persistently tried to obtain a grant to study Egyptology at Leiden University in Holland. Sometimes she would ask me to help her with her correspondence with the university, since she had little experience with email. She asked me to help her improve her English too. She loved Tutankhamun and Akhenaten, but she hated mummies. Once she had an argument with Zahi Hawass because he had authorized experiments on them. "How can you violate the sanctity of the dead like that, even if they are Pharaoh's people, who slaughtered the Jewish children and took the Jewish women into captivity?" she said.

She told me that she used to love the Pyramids but when she found out that they were large tombs for tyrannical kings, she said, "I don't like kings or tyrants or tombs but even so, when I feel sad and worried, I go to the Pyramids and my worries and pains vanish. They go and live in the stones of the Pyramids. They escape into the chambers." Once she invited me to a cup of tea and cakes at À l'Américaine on Talaat Harb Street. As she put sugar in my tea, she said with a smile, "I'm glad you've come back to Cairo. Many things were missing when you were away. Did you know that I always went to the Atelier du Caire in the hope of seeing you, and sometimes I went reluctantly to the Grillon. You know I don't like that place. It's all drinking and malicious gossip, and a woman is thought ill of if she so much as mentions the place. But I used to go with my friend

Afaf, who is more daring than me and knows well how to deal with those people. Imagine, she sits among all those men who are intellectuals and atheists and doesn't drink alcohol! Strange, isn't it?"

Then she said, "I want to know the secret of why you're so sad and distracted. To me you're an exciting person, just like the mysterious pharaohs. You know, you do look like a pharaonic statue—your forehead, your chin, your eyes, your wisdom." And I said, "All that? You're exaggerating. You should write poetry." Then she said, "Look around you and you'll see better." I said, "Is that advice?" She said, "I'm sorry, but I'm interested in you and I know you're different and sensitive and creative, and men of that kind are easy to hurt and to play with. I mean, don't give your heart to anyone who doesn't deserve your love, because your feelings are precious and refined, and many men misjudge women because women often lie and wear masks, and they have plenty to give but they give it only to those they choose and only when they want." For a moment I felt that she was hinting at something, that she liked me and was prepared to be with me. Or perhaps she wanted me to say that I was prepared to be with her and she wanted us to explore our feelings more, but I felt uncomfortable. I felt the weight of the moment and the weight of Hanan's feelings. At the time I wasn't prepared to have anyone in my life. I wanted to be me and to be alone. She felt embarrassed but she was happy with the confrontation and didn't fidget in her seat.

"Let's meet often," she said, "and I won't let you go until I've learned languages, culture, and humanity from you."

We laughed and I paid the bill, and then we left. It was raining outside.

"Do you know what my ambition is?" she said.

"To be minister of culture," I said.

She said, "To walk with you for hours in the rain."

Then I took her hand and we crossed the street, and I said, "God be with you. You sound like the poet Nizar Qabbani. He'll find you an answer."

Hibernia the Land of Rain

Chapter 4

"I am no longer young, and my heart, through weary years of mourning over the dead, is not attuned to mirth. Moreover, the walls of my cas tle are broken. The shadows are many, and the wind breathes cold through the broken battlements and casements. I love the shade and the shadow, and would be alone with my thoughts when I may."

Bram Stoker, *Dracula*

Dublin, 1998

I was waiting for someone to help me carry my bag, but no one volunteered. Aggrieved that I asked, one young man said my bag was my business, while a woman suggested that there were bags with wheels that didn't take so much effort to drag. Then she laughed. I would find out later that there was a scare about strangers and bags, which might contain explosives since terrorist operations were common, especially in Belfast in Northern Ireland.

Dublin didn't seem surprising at all. It wasn't as I had expected a European city to be. The streets were narrow. There were the modest English-style terraced houses, the old bridges across the little river, the simple shops, the children begging, the old people, and the impetuous young people, some of them Irish and some of them immigrants.

I waited at the bus station for more than an hour for the bus that would take me to St. Patrick's College in the town of Maynooth in County Kildare, where there was going to be a conference on Irish literature and its relationship with the concept of the land. I could hear Celine Dion's song "My heart will go on" from somewhere nearby. I drifted off to the sound of the flute and felt good about the world because I loved the film *Titanic* despite the tragic ending for the Irish poor. I passed the time reading the newspaper, which was all about the problems in parliament, the Good Friday agreement, and decommissioning IRA weapons in Northern Ireland. In front of the station there was a very beautiful hotel. I was drawn to the building, which suggested the style of the Victorian era. The old wooden entrance reminded me of the mashrabiyas and arabesques in the Hussein and Khan al-Khalili area of Cairo. The bus came and the passengers moved toward the door slowly and steadily. There were some reassuring smiles from other passengers.

I enjoyed looking at the plains, the valleys, the green hills covered in clover, and the streams. Despite the beauty, a cloud of mist covered the horizon, creating a sense that the end was nigh, and there were moments of the usual melancholy.

The sun had almost moved on to other lands but I could still make out what the town of Maynooth was like—a quiet town with houses no higher than two stories. The main street rose toward a large Gothic church called St. Mary's, with a tower and a large cross at the entrance. In front of it there was a large open space with a statue of the Virgin Mary in the middle and a gas station on one side of the road. The town looked quiet and different from Dublin, but I felt depressed because the town was full of old people. Young people were few and far between, even rare. I didn't see any children in buggies or walking next to their parents.

I asked for directions to the venue for the conference and they pointed to a large church, the church of St. Patrick, who drove out the snakes and became the apostle and patron saint of Ireland.

When I went down the drive the greenery on both sides was dazzling, strong, and imposing. The church rose high with its towers, its crosses, and its Gothic windows.

The gatekeeper led me to the church door and I met the person in charge of the conference. He didn't smile but told me to come with him. I followed in his footsteps, the echo of which pounded in my heart. We went up flights of stairs and came out on a floor close to the roof of the church; then he slid the bolt of a door. The light was so faint that I couldn't make out what kind of place it was. "You'll sleep here and we'll meet tomorrow," he said. "I live on the lower floor if you need anything, and there's an internal telephone in the corridor."

"Where are the other conference guests?" I asked.

"They haven't arrived yet. They'll be here tomorrow. You came early," he replied.

He left me and went off. I stayed alone in the room. I opened the window but could see only darkness. The greenness that had stunned me at the entrance to the church might as well have been ghosts and a bottomless sea of darkness. I was afraid. I closed the window quickly. Suddenly I heard the sound of approaching footsteps. I was delighted. I stood up to open the door in the hope of seeing someone, but I had a shock: there was no one there.

I sat on the edge of the bed. I looked at the ceiling and the walls, then, suddenly, the window burst open and a draft of air blew in. The sky rang out as if there were thunder and lightning. I quickly closed the window. I didn't know what had happened. Suddenly a shiver ran through my body and I felt a slight crawling in my scalp. "I'll read a book," I said. I felt hungry and cold. Then I said, "I'll go to sleep," and I turned out the light. I tossed on the bed. I felt that a hand was touching me. I opened my eyes and saw the window opening again. Someone had escaped through it. I shuddered. I cried out for my mother as I always did when I had nightmares. I sprang up and ran for the light switch. The room lit up. My heart raced and my mouth dried up as if I were in hell. I heard strange noises.

I ran to the window as fast as I could and closed it. I felt a hand touching me, a strange hand, soft and cold and hard. I screamed again, then rushed to the door and called the supervisor. But he didn't hear me. After a while he came to me calmly. I told him what had happened. He said it was the wind. I said, "No, it wasn't that. There were people." Suddenly a worker, who was one of the church people, arrived and made the sign of the cross on his chest. "The Lord bless our martyrs and our apostles," he said.

Then he asked me, "Did you hear voices too?"

"Yes, I did!"

So they're real. This place is haunted. I trembled like a young child and the supervisor was surprised. "I'll get in touch with the church security," he said.

"Who are they?" I asked.

"They're the spirits of the monks who taught here a while back. Most of them committed suicide or went to the sanatorium, and some of them disappeared and this place was abandoned. No monks or theology students came here any longer, so the church and the local council decided to convert it into low-cost lodgings." I remembered my friend who was studying at al-Azhar University in Cairo and living in the halls of residence. He told me how the halls were full of ghosts, especially when there was a power cut, and the students would shout out, "Awad, Awad"—the name of the ghost who was said to appear to them. It was also said that this Awad was an electrician who had been electrocuted repairing a fault in the wiring, or that he was a student who was killed in the dark by one of his friends because of an old vendetta.

His ghost continued to appear to the students whenever there was a power cut. And it became customary that they called out his name.

After the supervisor called security, they came of course, a man and a woman, and a state of emergency was declared. The man gave me a sympathetic look. The woman came up to me and patted me on the shoulder as if I were a young child.

"Tell us what you saw and what you heard," they said. I told them.

As I told the story, the expressions on their faces frightened me. I was alarmed that they believed me. So the ghosts were real.

"What do you want to do?" they said.

"I'd like to leave this place immediately," I said.

"It's late," they said, "and there's no public transport to take you to Dublin. A taxi would be very expensive."

"Never mind," I said.

The woman in charge of security called a taxi from her cell phone.

In a while it came. The driver was a lump of meat but he had a kind face and was cheerful.

"Where is he?" he said.

They pointed at me.

He looked and then said, "It's not their custom to appear to strangers. How did that happen?" Then he added, "You're obviously blessed and pious. That's why you heard those noises." I felt sleepy and exhausted and I just wanted to have people around me. I took comfort in their presence, especially the supervisor and the taxi driver, who said, "In just a few hours it'll be day and the weather now is cold, stormy, and rainy outside and I'm worried you might fall ill, because you're like a son to me. You can stay in the student halls in the university nearby."

The idea of staying in Maynooth was absurd, because there were ghosts, and there was the idea of Dracula with his teeth still buried in his victims' necks. But out of sheer exhaustion I deferred to their wishes, though full of fear.

Chapter 5

When I left Maynooth I didn't know what to do or where to stay. I was alone, with a heavy bag that was breaking my back, so I went to the students' hostel at Trinity College Dublin, where I was going to study. But I found that it was very expensive to stay there, at thirty Irish pounds a night. That was beyond my means. I left the hostel sadly. But I was delighted to see this ancient university, founded under Queen Elizabeth of England in 1592, and its fine old buildings and the statues in the middle of the campus.

I went into the university museum and saw the famous Book of Kells, the illuminated religious manuscript more than twelve hundred years old, once kept at the Abbey of Kells in County Meath.

I remembered my father, who spent a whole year copying out the Qur'an for an American friend called James, who was also of Irish origin. He was good-looking and generous and he would come to see my father every day with a bottle of mineral water and orange juice and sit with him for some time. He was amazed by my father's beautiful calligraphy, especially when he used the naskh script. My father would sit from after the dawn prayers until mid-morning and from sunset until the evening prayers copying out the Qur'an. He was like a hard-working Azhar student who has come from the countryside on a mission that he has to complete. James took the Qur'an and went to America and we never saw him or heard from him again. He told my father he was going to call himself Ahmed Ibrahim, but why Ahmed, and why Ibrahim? We don't know. I was stunned by the old library, and I also stepped onto the croquet lawns.

I went out of the university, had some fish and chips, and then called my supervisor, the head of the department, and told her I couldn't find a place to stay. She asked me about the conference and I said, "When I see you I'll tell you the story." She asked me to come to the university so that she could arrange somewhere for me to live. Then she invited me to her house and said, "We'll have lunch and then I'll take you to your new home." She was a large woman with hair that fell loose on to her shoulders, and although it was slowly turning gray it still gave her a feminine touch.

She had a way of speaking that suggested a strong personality, but she stammered when she became enthusiastic about something. Her eyes were kind, like the eyes of all compassionate mothers. She took a chicken out of the oven, saying she had cooked it before going to the university, and we ate it with mashed potatoes. Her son Raphael sat between us and suddenly began talking about *A Thousand and One Nights* and the genies that live in the underworld and in the seas and oceans. He said that Ireland and the Orient were similar in that they both believed in genies.

"There's a genie called the Witch of Kilkenny who lives in the mountains of Ireland and roams all over the country. And if you happen to meet her, she'll fall in love with you, and if she loves you she'll go around with you whatever you're doing. She's like life. She may give you everything, but in the end she'll get angry with you and take everything from you."

His mother looked at him and said, "Could you talk about something else?"

She may have felt that my mind had wandered and I had seen genies dancing on the window latch in the room. She sat down to share the meal with us, framed by the tresses of her fabulous hair. Sensing that I was tense, she said, "Would you like to hear some poetry?"

23

"Why not?" I replied. "A little poetry doesn't do any harm."

"There's a poet I love very much called Eiléan N' Chuilleanáin and I'm going to read you a poem from her collection *The Brazen Serpent*. It's called "Studying the Language":

On Sundays I watch the hermits coming out of their holes
Into the light. Their cliff is as full as a hive.
They crowd together on warm shoulders of rock . . .

Her reading was interrupted by the telephone ringing. "Sorry, an important call from my husband," she said.

My supervisor is also a poet. She comes from the city of Cork in the south and is married to a major poet. She's open-minded, loves the East, and hopes to visit Egypt. It was she who invited me to come to Ireland after we had corresponded for a long time online, since I was doing research into Irish literature, especially on the works of Seamus Heaney and James Joyce and their relationship to the land and the colonizer, comparing it to Palestinian literature and the poems of Mahmoud Darwish, in particular. She welcomed me and helped arrange my travel by writing to the Irish embassy in Cairo, which was refusing to let me travel on the grounds that I didn't have enough money to study. She gave me a chance to listen to the lectures and to use the library and other university facilities. She also asked me to translate some of the stories I write, so that she could read them. It was she who called my attention to the fact that there was a conference in Maynooth that Seamus Heaney would attend and at which he would read some of his poetry. I decided to travel a week early to attend the conference and meet him, and then go to Dublin, where I would be studying for a year. But because of what happened in Maynooth, I wasn't able to meet him.

Chapter 6

When I went into the house where I was going to live, accompanied by my supervisor, there was an old woman sitting alone on a sofa. I have always been afraid of old people and I run away from them, frightened of the way they look at me, which always makes me think of senility. I was filled with a sense of dread at that gray hair, which made me think of Noah's hair as he gathered his people together at the time of the flood. The smell of the tomb seemed to live in that house. It gave me bad vibes and I felt nauseous. My supervisor sensed how I felt and said, "Moataz, this is a temporary place while you look for somewhere else to live." Then she helped me carry my bags from her car to the hallway.

As soon as she had gone, the landlord and I went up to the room. He was a man in his seventies, but well-built, with severe features, a powerful voice, and white hair like his mother. He showed me how to use the gas meter, saying that you have to put in fifty pence to cook a meal and warm the room for two hours, fifty pence to use the electricity for a day, and fifty pence to have a shower. The more energy you consumed, the more you paid. I remembered reading in the Cairo newspaper *al-Ahram* that Ireland imports natural gas from Egypt through an underwater gas pipeline and that Israel also gets the gas very cheaply—"for a few shekels." When the man left, I closed the door behind him and felt the coldness of the North Pole run though my body. The loneliness was only the start of it. Homesickness was a ghost that had swallowed me up.

Harp Players

Chapter 7

As if I'm falling from the sky
Or the birds are taking me down somewhere deep.
The fall was noisy and violent.
That's how I was after you sneaked away from me
And your love spilled out on your treacherous ground.

My clothes were soaked from the pouring rain. I took off the coat that my mother had given me before I left. "Moataz," she had said. "This will ward off the winter cold." But she added in a warning tone, "Look after it, because it belongs to your brother, and bring it back."

I put the coat on the table halfway down the corridor and went to fetch a cup of tea from the cafeteria in the hope that it would warm me up and drive the smell of cold out of my blood.

On my way back, amid a crowd of students and visitors, I saw her: fair-skinned, shapely, with large buttocks. Her fatness was obvious, especially as she was wearing tight stretch trousers.

I smiled and made up my mind to speak to her.

"Are you sharing this table with anyone?" she said.

Without answering I stood up and made space at the table for her. I moved my bag and put it aside. She smiled, without giving me a chance to examine her. She was very friendly and asked me what country I was from. "From Egypt," I answered at once.

"Oh, Egypt," she replied with delight and surprise. "The Pyramids. It's my dream to visit Egypt."

I was filled with pride. I watched her as she ate her food, and listened to her, my hands wrapped around the cup of tea, which was getting hotter.

"My name's Simone. I'm studying music and I sing. I also run a choral group that's interested in world music. Its aim is to bring the peoples of the world together through music. We choose a song from every country and sing it at our concerts," she said. "Irish music is very similar to Arabic music," I said, "perhaps because we have shared in the same tragedy. We have long experience of sadness and suffering. The English, they destroyed us. I mean, they occupied us too." We went for a walk and relaxed, lay down on the lawn. She was happy. I had a strong desire to sing, so I sang. She seemed happy.

"You have a nice voice," she said cheerfully and with enthusiasm.

I felt more confident inside.

"I want you to teach me one of these songs," she said. Then she continued cheerfully, "I remember an Arabic song that my old boy-friend taught me. He was Moroccan. 'Ah, Zein, Ah, Zein al-Abdin / Oh roses in bloom in the orchards.'"

I laughed and said, "It's Morocco that will bring us to the world."

We left the campus. "I'm hungry," I said.

"Would you like to eat at Supermac's in O'Connell Street?"

"No," I said. "I want to cook for myself. I'm fed up with ready-made food. I miss my mother. She would always make me food, even in the middle of the night."

"All men love their mothers," she said, then added with a smile, "As do I," and we laughed.

We went to Marks and Spencer's in Grafton Street, a lovely street. Despite the crowds you feel that it's quiet and sad. We wander around the store. I feel frustrated. The goods stacked on all sides irritate me. "Consumer culture," I say to myself.

When we leave the store I look at the Romanian accordion play-ers. Their music breathes new life into me. My heart jumps in my ribcage and my spirit takes wing, hovering high, dancing on the lampposts in the street, and climbing up the awnings of the shops, then flying off and landing on the keys of the accordion, flirting with the fingers of the Romanian musicians, who laugh at me with their exhausted eyes and their reddish-brown complexions. We feel we are the children of one world. They play more enthusiastically, as if I'm their only child, as if I'm the only tender hand that feels for them in their exile. I throw them fifty pence and they smile. I nod my head at them in pleasure and the music follows in my footsteps, protecting my shadow.

Simone hurries off and I see her pedaling her bicycle, and her back and buttocks disappear into the crowd in William Street.

Before she went we exchanged telephone numbers and I told her, "You should only call me after noon, because I read till late and go to sleep after watching television for a short while." She assured me she would get in touch with me because she really wanted to see me. I felt that I existed again after the homesickness and that there was a woman who wanted me and wanted to be associated with me.

Chapter 8

The Beautiful Women of Dublin

When I started at Trinity College Dublin, I couldn't work out the university women. I couldn't tell whether they were conservative and shy, or whether they just didn't welcome friendship with a young foreign man. They didn't speak to me and I couldn't find the right words to start a conversation with them. Perhaps I was shy too; perhaps I had little knowledge of women or too many misconceptions about Western women—that they were easy and available, so why was it difficult to get to know them? The young women always rushed toward the library or the lecture halls. The cafeteria workers were kind and would often laugh with me, and when they saw me looking puzzled and lost they would do their best to set me straight, so I saw them as my friends. From time to time I would come out of the library to talk to them, drink tea or coffee, or eat an apple. Often they wouldn't take any money. "This is complimentary, for our Egyptian friend, who misses his mother so much."

Simone said, "You look rich, while I'm a poor peasant girl. I don't think I suit you, do I?"

She laughed as she said it, and then I wondered, "Why does she think I'm rich?" I tried to be open with her about my situation. I told her how I was short of money and I said, "I'm here to study, not to have fun." Yes, I wanted to meet her all the time, but didn't have time or money to waste and spend on her. I don't remember ever lavishing money on her. On the contrary, she showed an understanding of my circumstances, and realized that I was studying for a doctorate and that I needed help. She showed a generosity that embarrassed me. Once she said, "Yes, there are women who love a man for his money and think the man has a duty to support the woman in everything" but she was different, in that she had been liberated from the yoke of servitude and traditional ideas. Love was the only bond that tied her to her man. She advised me to get a job. I complained to her that studying took up most of my time, and that I had research I had to finish and I had to stay late reading in the library and photocopying the notes I needed, and that I didn't want to go back to Cairo without achieving what I had come to do, and that I loved life here despite the hardship, and that I had grown used to the way people behaved, and that I had started to gain some confidence in myself.

Simone met me near the university. She got on her bicycle and started to wipe the sweat off her brow. "The rehearsal exhausted me," she said. "The concert's coming up soon." She was always smiling. This time she was wearing a strange costume—a loose pleated green skirt and an embroidered red blouse. With her hair braided and wrapped around her head, she looked like a Bedouin or Gypsy girl. "I'll take you out to lunch," she said. "We'll have a Chinese meal—noodles, steamed rice, spring rolls, wheat soup with seaweed, shrimps with pineapple, and ice cream fried with honey, and we'll drink green jasmine tea."

I didn't comment on the menu, but I said, "The sky, the earth, the seas, and the clouds will work together to make this meal." Then I told her that I wanted to get a job, because I had spent most of my money, and if I didn't find work I would have to leave.

"Don't worry," she said. "You're not alone. Most of us are suffering. There's high unemployment despite the economic recovery and our membership in the European Union. There's only menial work, like working in restaurants and bars."

33

"I don't want to work in a bar," I said. "I don't like alcohol, God curse those who carry it and serve it."

"I'd be very sad if you left me and went back to Cairo," she said. "I've grown used to you. I'll try to help you."

Then, with her usual enthusiasm, she said, "Would you like to teach music?"

"Why not?" I said.

"You can give me lessons in Arabic singing, because I'm collecting songs from various parts of the world—from Nigeria, Spain, Costa Rica, Turkey, and Sweden—and I teach them to the group I run. I'll give you ten pounds an hour. Does that sound good?" she said.

"Better than nothing," I replied.

Chapter 9

The world is entire, and I am outside of it, crying, "Oh save me, from being blown
for ever outside the loop of time!"
Virginia Woolf, *The Waves*

I live in a small room that looks out on a back garden. It has simple furniture but what annoys me is that the bed didn't have sheets or blankets. When I mentioned this, my supervisor commented that she would sort it out. The room had a radio, and my neighbor lent me a black-and-white television that I would leave on all night to dispel the sense of loneliness around me and the phantom of the old woman. I stayed in this strange house long enough to get used to the cave of loneliness and the cold smell of my room. The electricity would cut out suddenly, or the gas would run out before the food was cooked, or the water would suddenly run cold when I was having a shower because not enough money had been put in the gas meter. I felt poor and needy, and sometimes mistreated by the landlord. I failed to pay the weekly rent on time because I had run out of money. I was waiting for my father to send me some of the money he had promised me but hadn't sent. The landlord was upset with me and started to scowl at me. One day he came up to my room and reproached me with a warning: "If you don't make sure to pay the rent on time, I'll throw you out of the room." I was determined not to leave the house and I called the police, who decided it would be best if I left the place straight away, but I asked for a delay to look for somewhere else, and they agreed.

On my daily journey I take the bus. I always sit by the window, looking into the gardens of the houses and at the daffodils, which look pristine and delicate. I remember my sister's young daughter, crying when I left Cairo. I go past Trinity College. I look at the clock on top of the building. The sky is very close, and rain is expected. I hide from the rain by sitting in Bewley's coffee shop drinking tea. I chat for an hour with an old woman in her eighties, and she tells me about Irish poets. She prefers William Butler Yeats and Paul Muldoon; she doesn't like Seamus Heaney and thinks that he's too interested in rhetorical flourishes.

She said that Yeats fell in love with her and wrote his *Rose* poems about her, as he did with Maud Gonne. I told her about Saad Zaghloul and de Valera and their secret letters about waging war on the English and throwing them out of Ireland and Egypt in 1916 and 1919.

I leave the coffee shop, cross O'Connell Bridge, see the women who sell flowers calling their wares, and I smile at them. They exchange greetings with me. I ask them if I can have my picture taken next to them and they pose for the camera. One of them isn't interested and another smiles like Marilyn Monroe. I wander down O'Connell Street, go into Eason's bookshop and browse the shelves. I go down to the lower floor and read for two hours, then go upstairs again and stumble upon many names and images. I'm drawn to the novel *The God of Small Things*. I'm amazed by the novelist and I wonder, "Is there a god for big things, big issues, and a god just for small things? Is she a Sikh, a Buddhist, or a Muslim?" Tagore and his poems, Gandhi and his wheel for spinning cotton, his thin, naked body, and his courage in the face of the oppressors. I was fascinated by Indian writers and their beliefs and by post-colonialist discourse. "They have the courage to discuss the relationship between religion and the state," I thought, "and between what is sacred and what is superstition. Salman Rushdie paved the way for them in *The Satanic Verses*, and let Ayatollah Khomeini's fatwa go where it wants."

I look at the book for a while, then decide to buy it.

I go out of the bookshop and walk past the General Post Office. I look at the statue commemorating the martyrs of the Easter Rising in 1916.

I remember the old man who met me by chance in St. Stephen's Green and began to explain the whole of Irish history to me as he wandered through the streets of the city with me, telling me the secrets of every building and the legend behind every statue in Dublin's squares. He finally stopped at length in front of the post office and said, "Here we lost many martyrs. Death counted for little compared with achieving independence."

Then he said, "I go past here every day and pray for them and see their souls hovering over Ireland at night, protecting it from its enemies and from the return of the English." "Don't think that all Irish people are patriots," he added. "There are traitors who would like to sell the country for a handful of coins."

I want to send letters to some of my friends, but I put off the idea till the next day.

I run into some refugees from Africa, Albania, Romania, and Armenia, as well as some Arabs. I am used to the Algerians and I recognize them easily, through the language they speak or the way they look, and they do likewise. They exchange greetings with me and say, "Welcome, Egyptian man."

"How did you know?" I said.

"We knew from your eyes, your accent, and your dialect, brother," they said.

"And you're from Algeria? Do you like Warda the Algerian?" I asked them.

"We like Abdel Halim Hafez and Umm Kulthum," one of them replied. "And Amr Diab—'O my love, light of my eye.'"

Then they started singing and I joined in. We talked about politics and the situation in Algeria, about the Islamic movement there. Then they talked about Sadat and his visit to Israel. I said, "The peace treaty was just his own personal decision. He didn't want another war."

And one of the Algerians, a man called Abu Alam, replied, "But what have you done with the land you recovered under the peace treaty? That's the big problem."

And I said, "Politics is a desert full of thorns and mystery. In general, we're better off in this state of peace than we were before. We've had enough wars and destruction. I don't have extensive knowledge of President Sadat's policy. I should read more about it, because he was assassinated when I was ten years old and the only benefit I have had from the peace treaty is the Fulbright scholarship that the United States aid program offers to academics in Egypt to develop their research. The struggle in Egypt is not only political now. It's also about how to make a living. We're struggling to survive and I think Ireland has the same problem. It's the fault of colonialism, which left behind incompetent regimes. Colonialism is gone from Algeria, but France is still there, as well as the neo-Islamists."

They listened to me with interest, but I didn't want to get any more carried away in case they got annoyed. "You're not at a lecture," I told myself, "Behave like a normal human being." I smiled at them and invited them to have lunch with me at home.

Abu Alam, the young man with the brown face, welcomed the idea and said warmly, "Why not? We'd like to try some Egyptian food." But the other man declined my offer, arguing that it was too late. So we made plans to meet up another time.

Chapter 10

The secret, shameful things are most terribly beautiful.
D.H. Lawrence, *The Rainbow*

Can I find fulfillment with a woman other than my beloved Siham? It's true that she has her own world completely different from mine, but perhaps we will meet one day. Simone is ready and prepared to make love and has opened all doors for me to possess her. She has surrendered all her keys to me and told me all her secrets.

After several meetings she said she was Catholic and sometimes went to church and confessed to the priest. But, embarrassed and with a smile, she said she had already known three men. Then she suddenly said, "I respect Islam. It preserves the humanity of women. Since I met you, I've been reading about the Islamic religion."

Then she said, "Moataz, I like you. You're kind and clever and cultured. Please forgive my previous mistakes. I'll start afresh." I was tense. So she had been reading about Islam because of me, but why was she interested in me?

Her voice trembling, she said, "Forgive me my reluctance to answer you on my emotional state when we started meeting. I was confused about my feelings because I hadn't completely ended my relationship with my fiancé. Now we've agreed on everything. I'll leave him the house and he'll give me some of the money I spent on renovating it. I think that should put you at ease so you can be sure I've completely ended my relationship with him, because we're totally different."

I think she misunderstood me. I didn't mean to get involved in an emotional relationship with her. Maybe the hesitant way I treated her brought her to that conclusion. I didn't mean for her to leave her fiancé or her lover. I just got along with her. She wasn't the woman I wanted. She was completely different from me. Yes, she was an artist and she was perceptive, but she was different. I tried to explain my point of view to her but she didn't give me a chance. Suddenly she hugged me in the middle of the street. She pressed her breasts hard against me and kissed me on the neck. I felt that people passing by, even those in cars, were looking at us. But I told myself it wouldn't be in good taste, or civilized or manly, when a woman embraces you, to lift her arms off and step back.

"Do you love me?" she said. I didn't answer. I looked far into the distance. She held me gently by the chin, turned my face, and looked at me lovingly. She reached into her bag and gave me some money. "This is for the taxi fare," she said. "I think you're late and you won't catch the last bus."

"And you?"

"I'll ride my bike. It saves me plenty of money. You should buy a bike," she added excitedly.

I was afraid to tell her straight that I wasn't skilled at riding a bike. I hadn't learned to do it when I was a child because my father was worried that a car might hit me and I'd be killed.

Whenever I felt frustrated and desperate, I wandered aimlessly through the streets and lanes. I looked at the shops, spoke to strangers, asked them the time of day in order to start a conversation with them, went to the river to look at it in the hope it would give me answers. I looked into the water. I marveled at how long the river is and at the boats that sail along it. I sat next to it for hours. I remembered the Nile and Qasr al-Nil bridge and October bridge at night, and the ships that sailed under them with dazzling lights and people dancing and singing on their decks.

At other times I would take the bus. Once, I saw a group of people standing in line at a bus stop. I didn't know the route but got on the bus and the driver asked me, "Where to?"

"Give me a ticket for three pounds," I said.

"Where to?"

I didn't answer.

"So you'll get off at the Sugar Loaf."

I didn't answer.

I preferred to sit alone. I looked at the farms and the houses. I tried to read but I couldn't. I thought I would read nature instead. I saw a high mountain topped by cloud. It looked like a volcano was erupting from the peak. I stood up and went up to the driver.

"I'd like to get off here," I said.

He looked back, then stopped, opened the door, and said, "Goodbye. Be careful."

He was smiling as he closed the bus door.

Did William Wordsworth, the great romantic poet who lived in England in the nineteenth century, ever come to these green pastures, I wondered? Did he write his poems in praise of nature in this place, next to the magic lake? Did Keats come here and see the nightingale, and write his timeless ode to her? When Gibran wrote *The Prophet* was he in this spot, coming close to the spirit of God? Was it here that the light that shines on nature came to him?

I crossed the road and saw some sheep grazing in a nearby farm. A young woman got off the bus with me. A car was waiting for her. I went up to ask her the way, hoping to speak to her and get a free ride. That was what happened, in fact. She agreed and her brother gave me a lift halfway up the mountain.

I started walking up the rest of the way. Against earth's gravity your body grows heavier.

I made a point of stopping people on the path to the top to talk to them and kill time. "You should hurry up before darkness falls," they said, and one woman warned me that I wouldn't be able to reach the summit before sunset. I had better go back because walking would take a long time.

I said, "I have to climb until I'm at least halfway up. I'm sure that at the top of the mountain you feel at ease, you feel free, you feel the spirit filling the place, you sense God in everything."

I heard a lamb calling me, as if it knew my name. I answered its call, imitating its voice—"Baa, baa"—and the lamb looked at me as if complaining that it was lonely. We struck up a rapport and I went up to it. There was no one nearby. Its eyes were looking at me. I think it liked my company and I too wanted to stay longer with the lamb. But I saw that the darkness was looming and I had to keep walking, so I left it alone calling out to me. My heart bled for it and I remembered that I had to keep quiet and move on so that it would forget me. On both sides of the path the flocks of sheep imposed themselves. I remembered Wordsworth and heard solitary Lucy Gray singing her sad song. I didn't reach the top of the mountain because darkness fell and I was worried about getting lost, so I turned back and had trouble coming down. I could see the lights of the small hotels and guesthouses at the foot of the mountain. I felt as if I were falling from the sky. On my way down I met a group of gypsies. They said, "Come with us and you'll find what you long for. You'll have the rest that you desire." They began to chant and sing:

> We are the men of the mountain
> And our women are our trees
> The nectar of paradise is what we drink
> And its flowers are our food
> Don't think about what the future may hold
> Because life is the journey of a wanderer
> And to rest is the aim of the migrant.

Then they lit fires and gave me some soup. One of their women passed me an apple and kissed me at the crossroads, and the taste lingered in my mouth for many weeks.

Chapter 11

"Warning: do not swim in the river. This river water is contaminated with rat urine, which may transmit Weil's disease. Anyone who falls into the river should consult a doctor immediately."

I read the warning posted on the embankment wall. I wanted to jump into the River Liffey. I felt a desire to swim. Perhaps this would lead me to the River Nile.

"Are you thinking of suicide?"

"No, absolutely not!"

The question took me by surprise, and I answered quickly. It came from a man who appeared to be over sixty. "Life is beautiful," he added, "and the most beautiful part of it is meeting nice people. Never tire of talking to people, and don't let a grain of hatred for anyone into your heart because love transcends death." He stopped talking and disappeared. It poured with rain and I hurried away from the river, into which the rats were jumping cheerfully.

Whenever I went into my house in Harold's Cross, I asked myself, "Will I die here?" because the old woman's eyes hinted at death and at how people decline from strength to weakness. I saw her whenever I came in or went out of the house. She sat on her chair and watched me, like the cruel fate that I expected would take revenge on me at any moment, especially when my sense of guilt and my embarrassment at my unjustifiable lapse into sin got the better of me. I thought she felt sorry for me in my distress and my loneliness because, like me, she was alone when her son went out with his wife. But I thought, "She's still alive, so this house does keep people alive. So let the days show us what they will do." I went up to my room and I heard a knock on the door. When I opened the door I found the landlord in front of me, shouting in my face, "I want you to leave. I don't want you in my house. You don't pay the rent on time. To put a long story short, I don't want Arabs in my house."

"Where shall I go?" I said. "And where shall I put my stuff? I've looked everywhere and I haven't found a room I can live in. The newspaper ads about places to rent never lead anywhere. I've called many landlords, but when they find out that I'm an Arab, they turn me down and say that the place has been let. I've also put an ad at the entrance to the university seeking somewhere to live, but no one has answered."

I almost cried, but I wanted to keep my cool in front of him.

Then I begged him. I said, "I'll pay the rent regularly and I won't make any noise at night. I'll always put coins in the gas and electricity meters, the old lady won't be aware of me moving when I come home, and I won't listen to loud music. I won't annoy the neighbors at night and I won't ask them for any help or to borrow any of their kitchen stuff, if that makes you happy. I don't want to spend the night in the street, and I beg you not to tell the department chair at the university so that she doesn't get upset at the way I've behaved and stop me studying in the university."

But he scowled and wouldn't back down. He retorted violently like some neo-Nazi, saying, "I don't want you in my house. The old lady's frightened of you and the way you creep about at night. The sound of your television terrifies her. Do you understand? I don't want you. Don't you understand?"

There's an old man who always stands next to the old woman who sells newspapers at the end of O'Connell Bridge, and who sees Moataz every day and says hello to him. Moataz asks the man whether he wants him to be around in spite of the fact that he's

Egyptian and a foreigner. "Ireland's big enough for everyone," the man replies with a friendly smile. The man says politely that he welcomes him as an honored guest in the country, since we are all guests. Although he suspects that the man is crazy because he's not standing up straight and his fingers and head are shaking nervously, he speaks like a kindly grandparent and looks as gentle as a child.

At night I walked down the street where I lived and imagined that the djinn were dancing on the branches of the trees in the form of terrifying ghosts. I had a sense of foreboding. I felt footsteps behind me so I hurried to put the key in the lock. The light dazzled me. My neighbor, the young man who lived on the ground floor and was always talking on the phone, was drunk this time. He smiled and put out his hand and said hello. Then he brought up the question of me leaving the house.

I asked him what the solution was, and he said, "I'll come up to your room right away." I arranged my room to receive the guest. I moved my suitcase aside, straightened up the sofa, and put my trousers away.

He came into the room swaying and I sat him down on the sofa. He was wearing shorts and a t-shirt. When he sat down the thick hair that covered his legs showed, but despite the hair his skin looked white and smooth. He smiled and laughed often.

"Would you like a cup of tea?" I asked him. "No, thanks," he replied. "I've had a lot to drink." Then he stood up and put his hand on my shoulder. His hand felt hot and I felt uncomfortable and tense. I gently invited him to sit down.

"He doesn't have the right to throw you out of this house," he said, swaying. "He hates Arabs and that's all there is to it. The Irish have become racists." He looked into my eyes at length. Then he stood up, looked around him, and said, "It's a really bad room. Why does he want to throw you out? It's no paradise!" He almost fell over so I stood up and took hold of him. He held my arm and almost embraced me. Then he announced, "You're a kind-hearted person." Then he said, "Get in touch with RTÉ Radio. Tell them your problem and they'll understand. But please don't tell him that I suggested this to you." Then he left. I watched him going down the stairs. I sat alone in my room, thinking about what had happened and packing up the rest of my belongings. I said to myself, "Should I speak openly to Simone about my problem and tell her I won't have anywhere to stay within a few days? Should I ask her for help? No doubt she would ask me to go and live in her place. Why has the devil tempted me with this idea? She isn't my wife and she hasn't yet ended her relationship with her boyfriend."

I tried to sleep but I couldn't. The room was bitterly cold and damp. It grew colder and my limbs went stiff. From my window I could see the sky clear of cloud, and there was no moon that night. I waited a long time for it but it let me down.

I put some coins in the meter for the electric fire. I moved the large sofa closer to the fire and let the warmth seep into my feet. The warmth spread through my body and through the window I could see apparitions leaping over the stars and swinging, so I wrapped myself up and fell asleep.

In the morning a tall policeman came, wearing a shirt as blue as his eyes.

"The only solution is for you to leave here," he said. "The man doesn't want you. What did you do to him?" I began to explain my position, who I was, what I was doing, and how I had struggled to get to Ireland. I told him about my worries that my supervisors would be angry and my fellowship would not be renewed. But he didn't seem to understand what I was saying. He left quietly after asking the landlord to give me three days' grace to find a place to live. I sat down in my room and was about to cry, and I remembered my mother.

I went to the university and met Joanna, the department secretary, a woman over sixty but still very vigorous. She was very sad when she found out what had happened to me with the landlord.

"Ireland is full of many people of this kind these days, although it wasn't like that in the past. I don't know what happened."

She promised me she would look for a place for me to live in the *Evening Herald*, which had a large section for real estate advertisements.

Then she suggested, "Why don't you go to the Islamic Center in Clonskeagh? It provides services to all Muslims and it also has lodgings for young people."

Then she gave me some letters she had received from the library and from the external mail.

"Look after yourself and don't be sad," she advised me. "Writers are always sensitive and suffer more than others, so don't lose heart. Don't be pessimistic."

As I was leaving through the campus gate to have lunch, I said to myself, "I won't leave this town. I'm going to stay in this place till I get what I want, even if I get evicted. I'll pester you until you open your doors to me or you know me properly, until you remove this shell called skin and get to know my soul. I will defy racism—that ugly word that the free people of the world have fought against, killed, and buried because they grasped the meaning of freedom and equality. Hasn't the blood of Christians and Muslims been shed to achieve equality? Didn't rivers of blood flow during the French Revolution and the Bolshevik Revolution? Have we forgotten the blood of Martin Luther King? So why do we have to keep talking about racism and practice it with such brutality?

The young Pakistani who met me in the mosque administration office asked for some money as an advance to book a room. Five Irish pounds a night. Then he handed me the key. "The mosque closes its doors at ten o'clock," he said. But I like to stay out late and I'm not interested in going to bed early, I said to myself. I'm a creature of the night. But then, to be religious means setting an example, and sleeping in the guesthouse next to the mosque requires commitment.

In the corridor leading to the administration room there was a bookcase full of books on Islamic law. I noticed an advertisement for a seminar on Sayed Qutb's *In the Shade of the Qur'an* and a trip to London to attend a Friday sermon by Abu Hamza al-Masri. In a corner there was a shelf with Qur'ans of various sizes and editions. There were also men with beards and women wearing the niqab who didn't speak Arabic. Maybe they were from Afghanistan or

India. Only the magical, nervous eyes of the women in the niqab were visible. "It's just like Cairo," I said.

Some of the young people smiled at me and greeted me the Muslim way. When I went into the room I felt I was in a hospital, not in a house. The walls were white, the bed was metallic and white, and the desk the same. To the side of the room there was a basin for washing. I felt no desire to stay in the room or in that place. I slipped out without asking permission from the management. I told myself that the money I had paid was a donation to the mosque, and I went out the back door.

I couldn't spend the night in the lodgings at the Islamic Center. I felt that I didn't belong there. I wasn't pure enough to live there.

Yes, at one time in my life I did want to be a sheikh or a priest, serving the mosque or the church and living in the sanctum forever. Or a temple priest whose only function is to serve God and the poor, to grow close to Him until one is completely pure and has become a Sufi or a mystic. I have always been tempted by the life of ascetics, those who carry their belongings on their backs, abandon life with all its bustle, go far away in groups that sleep on the ground, and share the salt, the bread, and the oil of the land. I never aspired to serve wine to my master, as Joseph's companion in prison dreamed of doing. But I did aspire to make wine that didn't make you drunk, and to wander around the cloisters of the temple or inside the mosque, alone but for my desire for God's love and compassion. I imagined life in a monastery on a remote mountain, living on subsistence until my heart learns how to be devout and my body grows accustomed to hardship, but so far I am still a person who carries his original sin with him and hasn't learned all the words necessary to make penance.

I thought of going back to the mosque, but argued that its remoteness from the city center was the main reason against it. There was also my fear of the darkness around the center, and the idea of being home by ten o'clock made living there impossible. My urgent desire to be free killed off the idea of staying there, so I decided to go back to where I was living, determined to fight the fanatical landlord. "Why does the world disown me like this?" I asked. "Why don't rooms welcome my presence? Why do even the streets reject me?"

It was raining when I left the mosque. I looked at the city through the bus window: the streets, the little houses, the electricity poles, the open spaces of green, the people rushing around with their umbrellas. I love life and this beautiful world, Cairo, Dublin. The bustle and the people. Despite the remorseless rain that caught me by surprise when I got off the bus, I loved it and felt that it was cleansing me and washing me. Ireland—the land of rain and fertility.

My Irish neighbor Brian, who was tall with red hair and a face covered with freckles, said, "This is the address of a woman whose house I used to live in. A good woman, and the house is surrounded by pine trees. You'll like the place, but please don't tell the landlord that I gave you the address or he'll throw me out as well." He asked me for the television he had lent me. I gave it to him and thanked him for his kindness. My young neighbor who lives on the ground floor was sitting in his room. When he saw me, he paid no attention, and I called him and asked him to help me pack my bags, which were so heavy they seemed to be laden with all the sins humanity had committed since Creation. He didn't respond. He treated me coldly this time, as if he was pleased I was leaving, as if he wanted to pretend not to be interested in me after the way I treated him on the night when he visited me drunk in my room.

Chapter 12

I went to Edna's house in Walkinstown. It was in a quiet street lined with trees on both sides. Spring had started to work its influence on the trees and the greenery was running rampant.

When I opened the door I noticed a dog sitting next to the stairs leading to the upper floor. It looked old and the place had a strange smell. I realized it was the smell of the dog with the sad dull eyes. The woman who received me was short with a pale complexion and her hair cropped short and dyed brown, and some wrinkles in the corners of her eyes. She was wearing a blue t-shirt and white bermuda shorts. I thought she was over fifty. She said hello and asked me to sit down. I felt at ease, even though I was in the kitchen.

"Egyptian. I'm studying for a doctorate in Irish literature. And I write stories," I said.

"I love reading stories and I don't know any Egyptians here," she said. "Those Moroccans and Algerians are all over Ireland now." We agreed on the rent—thirty-five Irish pounds a week, with two weeks to be paid in advance. She stood up and gave me a receipt for the amount. Then she said enthusiastically, "Your room's on the top floor." She went ahead of me upstairs to show me the small room, which had a bed, a desk with bookshelves above it, a fireplace, and a wardrobe. The room was nothing like my room in Harold's Cross, except for the window right next to the bed.

"You can study here in peace," she said. "There's no one but me and Mark, who lives alone on the lower floor. "He's mean," she added in a whisper. "He likes to have everything tidy. I think you'll get on with him though." As if she'd forgotten something important, she quickly added, "My daughter also lives in the room next to you," and she pointed to the room near the little bathroom. "She's studying computers and works in a gas station." Then she offered me tea and said in a warning tone and in a low voice, "You mustn't have anyone staying in your room for more than two days, and there's a mattress if you invite anyone to stay with you in the room, and you can watch television in the living room on the ground floor."

Who would come to my room when I'm here alone? Even in Cairo I wouldn't dare invite anyone to my house, because my father was conservative; no women and no friends allowed, on the grounds that houses were private spaces and if you wanted to meet friends you should do so outside. But Moataz wants to have friends to share his room and play with his things, friends he can read his stories to and listen to their opinions and their stories. Why not? Why doesn't he invite a girlfriend to his room? They would just talk and maybe she would cure his homesickness. In Cairo he would never dare invite a woman to his room. He wanted to remain the good, upright model, as his father labeled him. Because he was a descendant of Joseph, who conquered temptation and who wore a cloak that was pure, untainted by forbidden lust, like Adam before the Fall, and because what makes a man great is avoiding sins that would expose his private parts. Then he said to himself, "I have many books I want to read, and a big novel I want to write."

"Edna, pass me the shovel." When I heard his voice I looked into the back garden to see whose voice it was. "This is my friend who comes at weekends," she said. "He's a driver from the town of Monaghan. I've known him for five years." She started to tell me about him as if she were having an intimate conversation with an old friend she hadn't seen for ages.

The man came in, greeted me and said his name: "Patrick."

"I'm Egyptian and I'm called Moataz," I said.

"I know lots about Libya," he said.

"I'm Egyptian," I said.

Edna was washing the dishes. Then she asked me if I wanted to have another cup of tea, and complained about the state of the kettle. She promised she would buy another one soon.

"I've worked with many Arabs, especially from Saudi Arabia and Libya," said Patrick. "The Saudis are rich and the Libyans are too." More than other Arabs, the Libyans were very popular in Dublin, and Gaddafi was more famous here than anywhere else in the world. They think he's a real hero because he's the only one who's challenged the United States and the West, especially after the Lockerbie incident. They say he has his reasons to be hostile to some countries that still rule the world by brute force as colonialists.

Then he asked me, "Do you like Gaddafi?"

I didn't answer directly, but said, "I like literature."

As he drank his tea, Moataz didn't ask himself if he liked Gaddafi or not and he didn't ask himself if he liked the president of his own country or not. He knew that his brother liked the president and boasted that he had paved the way for a free-market economy. Moataz wondered, "Doesn't familiarity have a role in creating acceptance and even affection?" Because Moataz had grown used to the existence of his president long ago and he didn't know Sadat well. He had never seen him on a color television screen. He always saw his picture in black and white.

Then Moataz said to himself, "Why did Patrick ask about Gaddafi and not about President Mubarak?" Moataz often saw Muammar Gaddafi on the news, in his tent surrounded by his entourage and some camels dispersed here and there, watching a Bedouin troupe dancing and waving swords. It reminded him of Amr ibn al-As when he came to Egypt and stayed in Fustat. Moataz admits that he has tried to read the Green Book that Gaddafi wrote and that he bought at the Cairo Book Fair. It talks about setting up a socialist democratic republic based on justice, equality, and the fair distribution of wealth, about Arab unity and rejecting Zionist-American hegemony over the Arab world, but he didn't understand much of it, though he admired his heroic attitude in believing in Arab unity and his love for Abdel Nasser, even if some intellectuals have reservations about Gaddafi's restrictions on freedoms and the lack of political parties in Libya. He admired his son Saif al-Islam and his cousin Gaddaf al-Damm, especially for their daring and their desire to make reforms based on a new logic. Who will be the new leader? Saif al-Islam or Gaddaf al-Damm? "Blood-spitter," which is what Gaddaf al-Damm's name meant, was a strange name for someone so good-looking, but what does inheritance have to do with a handsome, well-dressed young man? Ruling is something else. We talked about Islam, about Egyptians and their manners and customs. He asked me about my women friends and how many I had laid since I had come here. Edna said, "Don't speak to my friend so much about such things." He must have drawn the conclusion that I was either conservative or shy.

Edna said, "Don't speak to Patrick about Islam because you'll give him bad ideas. Speak about anything else." What is it about Islam, Moataz wondered. What harm would it do to Patrick's mind if he heard me speak about it? When I spoke about the ban on sex before marriage or outside the framework of divine law, had I offended her by what I said? I didn't mean to turn him away from his own religion or proselytize. I was just answering his questions. Moataz didn't know why she had told him to refrain from talking about religion. Yes, he did seem enthusiastic, like a preacher perched on the pulpit, repeating word for word the expressions his father had learned at al-Azhar or that his father had passed on to him from his grandfather, who was the imam of a mosque called the Ganibkiya in the Migharbalin district. The grandfather had died while leading people in prayer. Moataz was on the verge of dissenting from these teachings and treating them with the critical mind he had acquired from his reading of philosophy and from his discussions with secular-minded people he had met in Egypt and abroad. From what Patrick and Edna said, he felt that he was talking about taboos or that it was a danger zone lighted by hell fire. He fell silent and wondered why she was so afraid of Islam, when he hadn't discussed or spoken much about it. I took my leave and went up to my room to have a rest. When I threw my body on the bed, I felt for the first time that I had a house that would protect me, and kind people to embrace me, and I cursed the landlord at Harold's Cross.

The days passed. I went to the university in the afternoon and stayed there till ten at night. The library staff always asked me to leave so that they could close the doors. I would hang around till the last moment, especially in the Lecky Library, but the staff generally showed great generosity and appreciation for work and scholarship. At first I was wary of them and thought I was being rather provocative when I sat to within a minute of closing time. But I started to understand the system and get used to it. A strong friendship developed between us. I started to prefer the Berkeley Library because it had the philosophy and Greek literature section and worked till the last moment, unlike the Lecky, where the staff were in a hurry to leave. Then I would go out through the old wooden gate of the university as if coming out of my mother's womb, from somewhere safe and contained into a world of wandering and loss.

I picked up my bag and wandered through the streets of Dublin. I went into bars and spoke to people in the streets. But I had to catch the last bus heading for where I lived, at eleven thirty exactly, otherwise I'd be forced to take a taxi, which would be very expensive, beyond my budget. I had come to this city at my own expense but at the invitation of Trinity College, and I had to arrange my own financial affairs while here. I was worried about spending everything I had left. I economized on food and drink and clothing. Even my shoes came unstitched and I hesitated to buy a new pair.

When I went into a bar, the people sitting there looked at me and knew I was foreign. In order to break the surprise of them seeing me and to overcome my own paranoia, I would deliberately speak to them and they would offer me a drink. I would say, "I don't drink alcohol and I prefer Coca-Cola."

"There's no Coca-Cola," says the barman. "There's Pepsi." I say that's ok.

My host promptly paid for the drink, and I thanked him. The Irish are very generous in bars. They become more human when they drink till they're drunk, but they have strange temperaments. By day they are practical, sullen, hurrying to work, and always worried about the morrow. But at night they frequent bars, talk convivially, laugh, and sing. In one bar I was asked, "Why don't you drink?"

"I don't like it," I said.

"Muslims don't drink, do they?"

I cannot lie, so I say, "God banned alcohol gradually."

"But the Muslims who come here drink and sleep with women. They do the same in Turkey."

"Turkey is the big problem in the past of the East and in its future," I said. Moataz didn't understand why he had said that. Did he hate the Turks? He had learned in history that the Turks were the reason why his country was backward. That's what the 1952 revolution had claimed, because it was the Ottomans who put an end to the Enlightenment Movement in Egypt, closed the modern schools, made do with just Qur'an schools, banned the teaching of the natural sciences, and sold Egypt to the English. They persuaded him that if it hadn't been for Abdel Nasser's revolution, Turkish rule would have weighed on Egypt forever. When the Islamic movement spread in Egypt, the Islamists tried to convince Moataz that the Turks were not Muslims and had nothing to do with Islam. Under Atatürk they adopted secularism as their new religion to please the West and joined NATO, and now they wanted to join the European Union. Hadn't they turned their back on their language and adopted the Latin alphabet in the belief that they would prosper by following the West? He also remembered that they hadn't allowed him to enter Turkey but made him spend the night at the airport when he was coming from Paris, just because he had an Egyptian passport rather than an American one. But didn't he have the right to find out the truth without falsification or prejudice?

My host in the bar said, "Do you know what the Irish are like?" I said, "Enlighten me."

"The Irish love to talk. They never tire of it," he said. "They always meet in bars. Don't hope to establish a lasting friendship with an Irish man or woman, because they are always fickle. Don't hope for more than one night, especially if you're a foreigner."

"That's a generalization and a stereotype," I said. "I have to experience people for myself, because they're not all alike."

"My children have all left. The eldest lives in Germany with her French husband. My middle daughter lives in Canada with her American husband. My elder son has gone to Spain with his Belgian wife, and my middle son lives alone in Portugal."

Edna had started talking about her family. She was talking as she busied herself washing the dishes piled up in the sink. I liked one china plate. I liked the color of the yellow flowers outlined in dark blue. She was wearing yellow gloves that matched the color of the flowers. It's like a giant puzzle, I said to myself. Every child in a different country.

"Don't you miss them?" I asked.

She took the gloves off and put some clothes in the drum of the noisy washing machine. "They've grown up," she said, "and they live the way they like. I tired myself out all my life bringing them up and now it's time to have a rest."

We left the kitchen and went into the living room, a quiet room looking out on the garden. It had a large fireplace, a television, a desk, some chairs, and a comfortable sofa in the middle of the room. Edna loved to relax on it from time to time. She leaned over the small drinks cabinet that lay in one corner of the room and took out a bottle of wine and two small glasses. She started pouring the wine, starting with the first glass. Then she raised her glass to me and said, "To friendship."

I raised my glass in turn but I didn't taste the wine. I stood holding it for a moment. She gave me a surprised look and stared into my face. "Religion, no drinking, I understand," she said. "You're strange," she added.

I told her that I didn't have any objection to sitting with people who were drinking and that not drinking was not based only on being religious, but for other reasons too. I wanted to stay in control of my mind. I didn't want to lose it. And I didn't need anyone else to feel sorry for me or to criticize me. I was well aware that if I got drunk many things would happen that I might regret when

I woke up and came to my senses. I convinced her that if I drink I would go into a state of depression and sadness, and a strange phase of crying and introspection may come over me, ending in me posing questions that don't have answers: about the universe, the creator, life and death, treachery, fate and predestination, and about women and men.

The room was faintly lit with candles spread around it. Edna was very fond of them. "They make me feel at peace and primitive," she said.

The smell of incense from a ceramic censer covered up the smell of the old dog. I don't know why but I asked her about the idea of her marrying her friend Patrick. In the way I framed the question I was careful not to appear to be intruding on private matters.

"We've never spoken about such things," she said. "Patrick used to be married and he has a son who's twenty years old," she added.

Patrick was at least ten years younger than her.

She smiled and, in a gentle, resonant voice, she said, "Would you like some wine?"

Then she looked at my glass and didn't repeat the question. "Ah, I've forgotten, other things . . ." she said.

"And doesn't your husband visit you?"

"Sometimes, when he wants to see his daughter Britney. We separated a long time ago. I wasn't happy with him. He was a nationalist and a member of a liberation group that was part of the IRA, and he went to prison for long periods. I bore the burden of looking after the children alone."

She stopped a moment, then picked up a yellow packet of Camel cigarettes. She opened it, pulled out a cigarette, and put it between her thin lips. Then she passed me a cigarette and I took it. Automatically, I picked up the box of matches and lit her cigarette for her. She cupped her hands around my hands. Then she blew smoke toward the ceiling and I lit my cigarette.

"Would you like to see a film?" she asked. Then she put on the film *The Piano*. She said how she adored the film and started to talk about the relationship between the sailor and the piano player and his love for her. The heroine loved to play the piano and wouldn't accept any substitute. She lived with her young daughter. The pianist couldn't speak so her daughter helped her to communicate with the world. The pianist wanted to sail somewhere with her piano but she couldn't find any sailor to move the piano for her, other than a middle-aged man. But he insisted that in return for his help she would have to play for him every day. The sailor fell in love with her. When her husband found out about this relationship he decided to put an end to his wife's temerity by cutting off her fingers, which were responsible for this betrayal, and this love. During the film Edna spoke about many things and suddenly I had an urge to wrap my arms round her, touch her hair, and feel the touch of her lips, but I was terrified of the situation. She drank a lot during the film. Her speech was slurred and when she stood up she almost fell over from the drink. I took her in my arms and embraced her firmly. She leaned her head on my shoulder and she was affectionate and warm.

"You're tense and tight," she said, so I hugged her harder.

"I'm as old as your mother and I'm not your lover," she said, in a voice that sounded like mewing. She patted my shoulder affectionately and said, "You can stay up as long as you like." Then she went upstairs to bed. When I went into my room, I said to myself, "I have to leave this place before I do something forbidden."

Chapter 13

At Cairo airport I pick up my bags. My elder sister is standing at the gate smiling. I am silent and sullen toward her. I have come back before finishing my mission in Dublin. Then I shout, "I want to get on the plane back to Dublin. I don't want to come back to Cairo." She laughs, pulls me by the arm, and says, "You have to wash your father and bury him because he's dying." This recurrent dream was interrupted by the sound of the telephone ringing, insisting that someone answer. I got out of bed, still lazy through and through, and incredulous that I was still in Dublin after this strange dream.

I picked up the receiver as I looked at my face in the mirror.

"Hello, is Mr. Moataz there?"

"Yes, I'm Moataz."

"It's Simone. Are you okay? I've missed you. I want to talk to you. I'll meet you at the university gates at five o'clock."

She didn't give me a chance to refuse or ask why she wanted to meet.

The rain was washing all of Dublin, falling in torrents. Fortunately I had borrowed Edna's umbrella, a brown one with black criss-cross lines. The umbrella had been lurking in a basket next to the door. I didn't usually like to carry an umbrella in case I forgot it, and it led to a quarrel. But for fear of catching a cold, I had to take it with me. I saw Simone next to her bike, waiting for me. I was half an hour late.

She greeted me with a smile and didn't comment on my lateness. Her hair was wet, as if she had just come out of the sea after swimming a long distance. I had a feeling I should kiss her, so I planted a kiss on her cheek. Then I held her to my chest. I felt good about doing it and she held me tighter.

"The group's agreed to let you teach us a new song, a traditional Egyptian one," she said, panting as she attached her bike to one of the metal bike stands that were common on campus. Then we walked toward the big croquet lawn that was set up two hundred years ago. The manicured greenness was magnificent and powerful. She looked at me with great affection, smiling from ear to ear. "Don't worry. We'll pay you for what you do for us: fifty pounds an hour. Do you like the offer?" She opened her diary and started to calculate the days, then made a mark with her pen.

"Would in two weeks suit you? Maybe the Saturday. I'll set the exact day and tell you," she said.

"I won't see you for two weeks?" I said.

She smiled, then said, "Of course not. We'll meet every day."

The idea of Moataz teaching them to sing was not his idea. But she very much liked his voice and the way he performed, and she loved the words that he translated for her. She told him he was very sensitive and had the ability to persuade others through his performance, even if they didn't understand the words. Moataz loved singing and felt that it was the only thing that could get him out of the loneliness and sadness that he suffered throughout his exile in this country.

He once sang her the Leila Murad songs "Ya habib al-ruh" and "Min baeed li-baeed ya habibi basallim," and although Simone wasn't beautiful she was kind and simple. "I'm a country girl from the town of Wicklow," she always said. "I'm not educated or distinguished like you. I'm not doing any research. I just love music and song. Singing and charity work are my life. I do lots of volunteering to help the poor and those with special needs. At the weekend I'm going to Wicklow to work in a bookstore, to sell books." Then she asked me, "Do you want any particular books? I'm free to borrow them or buy them at greatly reduced prices." "My doctorate's on poetry and politics," I said. "I love the poet whose poetry you're doing research on," she said. I gave her some of the poet's poems and asked her, "Read this poem for me, please."

The poem was *At a Potato Digging*, which is about the peasants who harvest potatoes and the troubles they face, the cold that freezes their fingers and toes on cold winter nights, about the disaster that struck when their potatoes were blighted after they had waited so long for the harvest, and about England's negligence toward them during the Great Famine of 1845 to 1852. Simone said with emotion, "This famine wiped out a million innocent Irish because of the blight that hit the potato crop, which at that time was the staple food of the Irish, and then they fell ill because of malnutrition, and thousands of them caught typhoid, cholera, and diarrhea, and died of hunger on the death ships to the United States, and the British authorities left them to die of hunger, or to drown in the sea when they tried to escape to America or to some nearby country." Then she added sadly, "Half of my ancestors died in this famine. We won't forget the dead. The sadness in our hearts is an eternal monument, like the Pyramids with you," she said with emotion. "In the heart of Dublin and on the banks of the River Liffey in front of the Customs House there are statues commemorating this tragedy, which still lives in our consciousness."

Then she went back to reading the poem, by which she was moved yet again. She explained the poem to me at length and made sure I understood.

Then she said, "It's as if Heaney is speaking for me. I also have feelings toward the earth. We have the same village roots, me and Heaney, I mean. We're simple country people who can understand and describe nature, not like city people who have been corrupted by noise and conflict."

We had a coffee, came out of the university cafeteria, and linked hands.

Chapter 14

I took along some white carnations I had bought from the Spar supermarket for two pounds. The flowers had called out to me and begged me to buy them, so I did, although I didn't want to give the visit a romantic quality or ask for more physical intimacy. Flowers do bring people together physically and enable the language of emotions to come into play, rather than the language of reason. That's why they have become the language of lovers, the language of harmony and sentiment. I read the address: Rathgar, Garville Street. There were houses regularly lining both sides of the road and trees quietly declaring their presence. This was the house. I stepped forward. The gate was closed. I called out her name. She stuck her head out of the window. She smiled as usual and told me to come up. The gate opened by itself and I went upstairs.

She was alone. She took me to the living room and sat me down on a comfortable sofa. The piano took up a substantial corner of the room and a candle, single like me, lit the place, standing in a silver candlestick on top of the piano. I looked at the ceiling and saw that it was like a sky studded with stars, in various shades of blue, a loud blue, and a sad blue. There was a bookcase with a fair number of books, a large stereo system that was playing soft, sad music, an endless number of records, a bookcase that took up part of the wall, some pictures, and some wooden chairs. She sat down next to me, cheerful. I didn't look in her eyes, but at the ceiling, and then I gazed into infinity. Her voice interrupted my sense of feeling lost. "My old boyfriend painted it by hand. For two months he did nothing but this ceiling," she said.

I remembered Michaelangelo and the ceiling of the Sistine Chapel.

"Did he love you that much?"

"And more than that!"

"And what happened?"

"Politics messed up his mind. He dreamed of a united Ireland and the English leaving Northern Ireland," she said. "I like politics, but I don't trouble my mind with it. I prefer to sing and I think it's the driving force behind the universe. It can bring about change, and not war. Do you see what I mean?"

We spoke much about music, about Beethoven, Bach, and Irish folk music.

Then I plucked up courage and asked her, "Does he take part in terrorist acts?"

"I don't know. We don't discuss things like that here. If anyone knew I was talking to you, I would be killed or buried underground. We don't have the luxury of talking about the country and what happens in it."

"I want to hear you play," I said.

There was a violin resting on a seat nearby.

She passed me a glass of red grape juice and said, "I spent the whole day cleaning the house in honor of your visit. I don't like cleaning or preparing food, but I did these things for your sake. I'm a very good example of a modern woman. I always eat out and, as you can see, I'm single. My boyfriend and I have split up and we sleep in separate rooms. It's only the place we have in common and we'll soon sort things out. We're now discussing the idea that one of us should let the other have the apartment. This is his apartment, but I paid a large amount of money to renovate it, as I mentioned to you earlier." I looked at her and understood.

"Since you came into my life I've decided to take positive steps as far as my relationship with him is concerned. I know you hate duplicity. You like people to be candid and not to betray others. You don't approve of anyone sharing my body or my soul with you," she said, then stood up, went to the table, picked up some candy, and offered it to me. It was pieces of chocolate in the shape of broken hearts. I hesitated to take one. I was afraid of their color. Those brown hearts that had been killed by loneliness. I wasn't afraid of the chocolates but of what was inside them. Perhaps it was poison; perhaps she wanted to kill me. I'm always wary of women like that. Beautiful creatures to look at, but being intimate with them is hell and madness. I wasn't afraid of intimacy, but really of poison. That's what my mind imagined at the time: the evil woman. I was afraid I wouldn't be the same again.

She took my hand between her hands. They were cold. She said, "Your hands are soft and warm, and your eyes are deep and brown." Then she asked me what color her eyes were.

"Amber," I said. "The color may change in sunlight."

I felt exhausted, as if her emotional outbursts had weighed me down. I couldn't tell her straight that I still didn't love her, or that I desired her, or that I was attached to another woman in Cairo. Then, in a voice full of sympathy, she said, "Moataz, you're innocent and sad, and that's what attracts me to you. I want to shake the sadness and the homesickness out of you. Give me a chance to do it."

I reached out to clasp her hand, out of a desire to connect. Inside me I felt a desire to make her happy, if only for a few moments. I yielded my fingers to her. I moved closer. My heart pounded, and the lust made my blood pressure rise. There was a tug of war between the desire to go all the way and the desire to stop at a certain point. But my beloved Siham appeared on the ceiling of the room with her silver wings, and I imagined her tears falling on me. They drowned me and brought me to my senses and dispelled any desire I had to have sex with Simone.

I took my leave, saying I hoped to be in touch. I went out, leaving the piece of chocolate next to the solitary candle on the piano cover, and went down the stairs.

I walk along the road, alone and lost, like Leopold Bloom in *Ulysses*. I remember my first love: she has the eyes of every woman and the tresses of her hair are the lifeline that always saves my soul from falling into a relationship that my heart and my mind wouldn't approve of. Although she has married someone else, she still lives in my heart. With her voice, she traces the world of sorrow in which I still live.

My friends say: "You're mad because you're living your old delusion." I often call her on the phone, listen to her voice, and then hang up. She says, "Hello, hello," like a divine melody that graces my ear for many days. But she's married now and you have no right to her. That's how I justify my deprivation and weakness to myself. At that point, I remember Simone and the future of my relationship with her. Then I make light of the subject to myself and say, "I didn't come to Dublin to fall in love. I came to study."

Chapter 15

"Moataz, you're only a lodger here. What you pay covers only lodging, it doesn't allow you to steal food. Please don't touch the fruit and other food in the fridge. This isn't appropriate behavior."

I found the message stuck to the table in a corner of the kitchen. After that, messages became the method of communication between me and Edna, who I didn't see often.

I had in fact devoured her bananas. I was hungry and couldn't find anything to eat while studying at night. So I went downstairs, afraid of the ghosts that lived beyond the window in the kitchen garden. I remembered how my mother used to make me fresh food at night and say to my brothers, "Moataz is working hard and needs to be well-fed. Moataz is frail and street food makes him ill."

I cried alone in my room. I soaked the pillow I slept on. I wrote my mother a letter, complaining about Edna.

I become possessive about my food. Edna had taken food from me but didn't like to give back. She was selfish at times and generous at others, but she taught me the culture of asking permission. I did in fact pay only for lodging and not for board. She was a single woman and lived off my rent and on welfare money from the government. She too was scraping by, paying off the debts in which she was drowning. Even the house she lived in was not completely hers; her children owned a share of it. She had to pay the mortgage, so she had agreed to rent one room in the house to me and another to Mark.

Her fat friend Julie, who had been her friend since they were in the orphanage together, would visit her from time to time. Edna said that she was the only friend in whom she could confide a secret, and that the two of them had escaped the orphanage in a village in County Cork. They were hungry and afraid and Edna miraculously escaped being raped. Three outlaws had attacked her. She would have bled to death had it not been for the people of the village they had gone through, who called the doctor. When she had recovered, they walked from Cork till they reached Dublin. There, her friend met the owner of a bar, who gave them work cleaning the bar. Edna soon became a waitress there and at that time she met her husband. She wasn't aware of his political activity but she was very helpful to him. She allowed him and his friends from the IRA to meet in an inside room at the bar, and when the owner found out he fired her. Then a government decree came out banning her from work in any government job because she and her husband were implicated in a bombing at a London train station in 1973 during the time of the Troubles.

I approached the Bank of Ireland. There was a line of people. I took my place, watching the girls' legs and the men's faces. While I was looking at the screen of the ATM, the people's voices overlapped. They didn't look away when I looked at them. On the contrary, they showed me the same interest in return. I took my Visa card out of my wallet, ready to put it in the ATM. "The Bank of Ireland welcomes you," I read on the screen.

I could hear bits of the conversations coming from behind me:

"He's going to the Kitchen Nightclub."

"I'm doing research on racism in Ireland."

"She's a whore."

"My friend's going to America. He won a lottery. He's going to join 44 million other Irish people there."

"The foreigners are everywhere in Dublin."

"Fuck off."

The Bank of Ireland offers you all banking services.

Please insert your card.

Insert your PIN, then press ENTER.

Enter the amount required, then press ENTER.

Please wait.

We regret that the withdrawal transaction cannot be completed.

You do not have sufficient funds.

Please withdraw your card.

I had spent most of the money I had, and only a little remained.

I wonder: is there any use in this trip, this exile? I left my country, my friends, and my family to come here. I always felt homesick, especially among people. I experienced racism in Ireland and I hated it. Someone hits you on the cheek. You shout out, but at the same moment you find a woman, or a man, or a boy, or a girl coming up to you and saying, "Don't take any notice of him or her. We're not all like that." You're talking about racism that's here! Doesn't it exist throughout the world, even in your country? Or does homesickness amplify the way you feel about things? You're the only person who can talk about racism: isn't Nubia completely isolated from Cairo? Aren't people judged by appearances, by the color of their skin, what model of car they have, and how smart their clothes are? Aren't you persecuted sometimes because your name suggests a different religion or a different ethnicity?

Even you, when you talk, people don't understand you. People speak the language of money and necessity, while you speak the language of culture, change, acceptance of the Other, and diversity, and they look at you and laugh. Perhaps they accuse you of being mad or being perverse.

Does it matter that I'm here? I could have stayed in Cairo and continued my research into Irish literature. And why Ireland in particular, anyway? Yes, I longed to walk down its streets imagining myself as Bloom, the hero of *Ulysses*, as he goes along the streets of Dublin looking for his identity and proving to the Irish, even by arguing, that a country is the place where you live and where you identify with the other inhabitants regardless of religion, culture, or ethnicity. Or else as Stephen Dedalus, the young man seeking the truth, seeking his roots, his psychological and sexual identity, the young man who is tormented by desire and who struggles to understand the idea of true religion. I'm different from them. I've come to Dublin because I was fed up with being in Cairo: the constant crowds and pollution, the exhaustion, the inability to achieve anything, the obstacles to everything, the constant arguing at home with or without reason, and my brothers' interference in my way of life.

Conditional freedom in Cairo. I thought that leaving for Dublin was a chance to explore my identity and my roots, away from all these influences. I thought I would be me.

I stay up late at night, watching television or reading literary classics. I'm completing my education. I'm also reacquainting myself with international cinema. I'm addicted to watching Marlon Brando movies, especially *A Streetcar Named Desire*. I long for my beloved in Cairo, so I write a poem to her every day. My longing for her has made me take up poetry. She is my muse, the angel that inspires me to see the most beautiful images and to write these lines:

In the darkness of the tunnel through which I've been walking
Since I was born,
You were the sun and the tree at the end of it,
And you were always my destination

I dreamed she had come into my room. She found me asleep on my bed, which is only big enough for one. She kissed me on the forehead, then she put her moist lips on one of my eyelids. Her fragrance triggered the springs of desire; this feeling overwhelmed me. I was angry that my platonic feelings had degenerated into lust. As she kissed me, her hands touched me down below. Then she pulled back and said, "You desire me." She moved away from me, saw that I was embarrassed, and she laughed. Then she came back to me, bearing the desires of all women. Then she lay next to me for us to make love.

Her hair is so long and thick that it envelops me. Her smell penetrates all my pores. Her eyes send me to worlds of magic and desire that I have never tasted before. I said, "You have lit the way for me and traced for me a world of light where I can live. It will fill me forever." And the room filled with light from her body and I saw light above me, and light below me.

I said, "I want to be a real presence in your life." She didn't respond. She looked at me with wandering wistful eyes. Then she said, "The day when you are in my life I will lose you forever. So let's stay always as we are: I invoke you and you invoke me."

I said, "I invoke you, but you don't invoke me. Where do I fit into your love and your interest?"

She said, "The proof is my body, which belongs to you."

"No, that's not enough," I said. "I want your soul."

Suddenly a little girl screamed. I saw a woman who was slightly plump and a brown man who looked like someone from the Caucasus. She pulled away and freed her hair from under my arms. She kissed the palm of my hand and left. She took the light with her.

In the morning I felt happy. I went into the bathroom and cleansed myself. The weather was cold. I felt full of joy for the next two days.

Chapter 16

*Let my Ba soul come forth to walk about hither and thither and whithersoever
it pleaseth. Let my name be called out, let it be found inscribed on the tablet
which recordeth the names of those who are to receive offerings. Let meals from
the sepulchral offerings be given to me in the presence [of Osiris], as to those
who are in the following of Horus. Let there be prepared for me a seat in the
Boat of the Sun on the day wheron the god saileth. Let me be received in the
presence of Osiris in the Land of Truth-speaking—Ka of Osiris Ani.*

The Papyrus of Ani, *Book of the Dead*

Whenever the bus went through Harold's Cross, I noticed a large
iron gate and a long driveway ending at a church. On Saturday and
Sunday every week I saw hundreds of people—old people, young
people, children—going though this gate, and I asked a passenger
who was sitting next to me, "What's behind that gate?"

"It's the cemetery," he replied.

One day I decided to visit it. The bus stopped and I headed
toward the iron gate into Mount Jerome Cemetery. I bought some
flowers. The caretaker rushed out, saying, "It's too late. We're going
to close the gate at exactly five o'clock." I looked at the clock and
said, "There's still plenty of time, fifteen minutes." He smiled at me
and went back to his lair.

I made my way down the driveway. The weather was relatively
mild. For the first time, I felt calm and at ease. The sense of homesickness had gone. I smiled when I saw tombs in the form of
pyramids and obelisks.

I put the flowers on one of the graves and recited the Fatiha. I remembered family and compatriots who had died. I found out what death meant when my younger brother Hussein died. He was four years younger than me. He had dehydration; he wilted and died. He was beautiful, with big almond eyes and snow-white skin, flecked with red. He laughed and had fun and played. He had just started walking and would often fall, so I would hurry to hold him. My mother would tell me off, saying, "Leave him, he's young." When my father beat my mother, she left the house. In order to punish him she left without Hussein and without me. We stayed at home with my father. He didn't know what to do with us. Hussein developed a fever and diarrhea and lost his fluids, then went to rest in peace forever. I still remember my father carrying him in his white shroud and going down the stairs, while my mother and I wept for him and screamed. I learned how to weep at an early age and it has never left me since. As for my mother, she now atones for her guilt by giving me and my brothers more protection and love. She always remembers Hussein and cries when she does, and insists on visiting his grave on feast days. I've never gone with her because I'm afraid of spirits and of the djinn.

I don't know why, but I also remembered the tomb of the unknown soldier in Nasr City in Cairo, which I always go past on my way to work and where I always recite the Fatiha for the martyrs who sacrificed their blood for our sake. The unknown soldiers are not unknown and their souls flutter around the Egyptian flag, preserving it from defeat and humiliation.

I remember Ali, my aunt's young and handsome fiancé, who came from the Khadra estate in Agamiyeen village in Fayoum and who died fighting in Sinai. There were only a few weeks to go before he was to marry my aunt, but he was killed. He looked like a young Irishman, with his red hair, freckled face, and short stature. I thought of my sister's daughter, who fell into a canal while playing and drowned in her short white dress, while her father was dozing in the garden. I strolled between the tombs and read the gravestones. "Here lies the Irish hero who died defending his land. The English killed him in Croke Park Stadium in 1920."

What if I died now? What if one of these tombs opened up and I fell into it? Who would save me and who would pull me out?

Death, the torment of the grave, and the bald snake! What will I say when the last trump is blown? What will I say about myself? And how will I explain my deeds on the Day of Judgment?

Hell is for those whose deeds have been the biggest failure, those whose efforts have been wasted in life, though they thought they were doing good deeds. They will be given water like molten brass, which will scald their faces, and have pus to drink.

And the Zaqqum tree with a sheath of flowers that look like the heads of devils, and the accursed tree, and molten lead, and iron and copper, and no one will receive help other than those to whom the Lord shows mercy.

On the other hand there is Paradise or the room where there is happiness and inner fulfillment, comfort for eternity and rivers of pure honey and wine that does not change in color and does not make you drunk, or sick, or dizzy. There they are served wine in cups from a spring, white and delicious to the drinkers, *No bad effect is there in it, nor from it will they be intoxicated.* And there will be abundant supplies of many fruits that are neither out of reach nor forbidden, and houris and women of modest gaze and boys made eternal, and figs and olives, grapes and palm trees, and shade, and the lotus tree in the seventh heaven with noble angels on it praising God night and day without flagging or failing.

And where am I in all this?

How I need the *Book of the Dead*, the eternal book of the Pharaohs, in my exile, in the hope that it might be a comfort to me on this long and uncertain journey. My father always said that his grave would be illumined by the light of God, which draws its light from a lantern that is like a brilliant star fueled by a holy tree, an olive tree that is neither in the east nor the west, because he was a faithful servant of God and because he recited the Qur'an, especially the Rahman chapter.

I came out of my reverie to the cawing of a crow that had landed on the branch of a tree. Darkness began to shroud the cemetery square. The clouds grew gloomier and anxiety and fear crept into my limbs. I was afraid the bodies might come back to life and I imagined that the caretaker had locked the gate and gone, leaving me alone to live with death. I regretted having come here in the first place, because cemeteries are not to be taken lightly and if you visit them, it should be in daylight. I recited the chapter of the Qur'an that starts *You are distracted by competition for worldly gain* and hastened my pace, as if the spirits had risen from their resting places and started to come after me, breathlessly asking me to open the exit gate for them too. I began to shout, begging the caretaker to show his face and respond to my appeal. I almost fainted when he didn't reply, and I could hardly breathe.

They said she had lost her mind and picked up men as hungry birds pick up seeds, that she took them to her room every evening, and that she stood there and invented strange stories to attract their attention. Her hair, which fell to her shoulders, her strange and mysterious eyes, her amazing bronze skin, her perfect posture, and her optimistic smile all drew men to her. She told them she was single and that nobody called her or spoke to her. She spoke to them about the sufferings and isolation of being a stranger, and they would follow her as if they were sleepwalking. She said that love had disappeared from the world and that planting it in people's hearts was now too much trouble. I imagined I had seen her more than once in Eason's bookshop buying novels or *al-Hayat* newspaper, or sitting for hours in the park in St. Stephen's Green looking at the greenery and the flowers or the geese that hide from the cold in their little boxes. She wears a dark coat around her shrunken body and looks distractedly at the world.

In the evening I saw her in Temple Bar, smartly dressed, like a country girl wearing an embroidered skirt or like a princess newly crowned, walking alongside a young Irishman who looks like one of the faces in the Fayoum portraits.

McNees, the owner of the shop where I buy things in Dame Street, told me that he knew this woman, and she was an Egyptian who had been studying Irish literature at Trinity College some time back. He said she was called Dalia and that she was very beautiful and eccentric. Sometimes she would drop in on him to buy things, leaving him with stories about her distant country, smiling at him breezily, and looking at him in a way that begged for understanding and communication. At other times she would walk by grumpy and depressed. She wouldn't speak to anyone and would let it rain on her hair and her clothes, even though she was carrying an umbrella in her hand that might have protected her. McNees would look at her through the shop window, wanting to call her in and ask her what was up. But she wouldn't take any notice of anyone. She would keep looking at the sky, which was throwing its tears on the dry land in abundance, as though she could see the clouds taking on the shape of vast pyramids and the sun shining despite the fog and the thunderstorm louring in the sky. McNees described her strangely beautiful face and how her hair was as black as the darkness of dreams. He spoke of the ring of her voice and the way she walked. He described her eyebrows, which looked like Nefertiti's eyebrows, and I realized it was her. He said, "I fell in love with her despite hardly knowing her. I myself waited for her every day in the hope of meeting her and making friends with her, although it was impossible she would be where I expected."

She would buy a lollipop, candy, and many postcards of various parts of Ireland from him. She spoke at length about her father, who had sent her here—where there was learning, a cold climate, and a conservative environment. He had forgotten that being alone could only lead to liberation and maybe madness. He took a banknote out of his wallet and said, "She told me to keep this note forever." Then he gave it to me and the writing on it was in Arabic.

The sky is blue
And the sun is like amber
And my heartbeats are a gong
Announcing the passage of time
And the river flows in my veins
And empties into the well of oblivion.
The memories and pains

Will definitely be swallowed up by time.
So remember me forever.

McNees admitted he fell in love with her as soon as he saw her. Once he went with her to her house, and he felt very sorry for her when he saw the state she was in. He asked me if I knew her family in Cairo, and if I did, he said I should get in touch with them, so that they could come and save her from the appalling state she had reached. While he talked to me he was handling orders from other customers, for cigarettes, chocolate, bottles of milk, and packets of chips. I myself picked up a packet of Chiclets and started to fiddle with it in an attempt to escape the difficult situation I had put myself in.

McNees was a portly man with a red face and eyes as green as the Dublin pastures after rainfall on a sunless day. He often smiled at his customers. I couldn't explain to him that it would be difficult for me to talk to her, that it wasn't my responsibility to write to or contact her family, and that my sympathy only went as far as feeling sorry for her and looking on thoughtfully. I didn't want to hear any more. I wanted to walk down Dame Street, go to the ancient castle there, and imagine myself as some medieval warrior fighting for his country or to rescue his beloved from the clutches of invaders.

Abu Alam and I started to wander around the city together. We would visit the stores. Many of the tourists, especially the Scots, would ask us the names of bars. They wore their national dress— tartan kilts, white shirts, sporrans hanging over their private parts, long socks, and shoes of thick leather.

Abu Alam commented, "I swear those young men don't wear underpants." I was surprised and said that the cold air would easily get through to their bottoms, and we laughed.

We walked as far as the Savoy Cinema, which was showing *Dancing at Lughnasa*, a film based on a play by Brian Friel and starring Meryl Streep.

I remembered Siham—the first time I saw her and the moment I fell in love with her. She was playing Ophelia in *Hamlet*, and I was infatuated with her from that moment. But she hadn't given me a chance to declare my love, and then she got married. I was frustrated when I found out. She didn't suit him, it seemed to me. She suited me perfectly. I wrote about her often. She was delighted with the stories I wrote, but that didn't bring about any kind of communion. When I later saw her ex-husband, who was a journalist friend of ours called Sameh, he said, "I read your story. You made Siham into a legend. You'll be her victim like me. You don't know her well. The decision to marry was her decision, and the decision to divorce was also her decision. When she got pregnant by me and I tried to approach her amorously, like lover to lover or a husband to his wife, she jumped out of her seat and said, 'Your role's over now. I have what I wanted and you're no longer any use to me.' And she went off to her mother and left me alone."

He was like an actor performing a tragic scene. He said, "You've been deceived and dazzled by what she writes and the roles she acts, or perhaps captivated by her beauty. I think that writing and theater are her life, and she uses everyone she knows as material to write about. Madness is that woman. Don't hover around her too much as she will burn you." He was desperate and lonely. I wanted to take my leave and go home, since it was late. He asked me to stay or to invite him to my place! It wasn't the right time. I left him in Tahrir Square. I tried to weigh it up. "Is the woman I love evil," I wondered, "or is he doing her an injustice?" That's how it always is: when lovers part, one of the two sides has to be nailed to the cross while the other one throws the stones.

Abu Alam took me by the arm and said, "A penny for your thoughts."

We went to have a coffee in Bewley's.

On the way back I saw the General Post Office building. I bought some postcards and sent them to my friends in Cairo. Most of the cards portrayed the Irish countryside, with herds of goats led by shepherds, or a modest country cottage with booze bottles lying on the ground outside. The doors of the houses were always painted red, white, yellow, or the color of the sky.

I was drawn to a card with a picture of the statue of Molly Malone that faces Trinity College and that has the story of the woman written on it.

When her friend invited me to a drink in the Cherryfield bar in Walkinstown, Edna sang the epic lament for Molly Malone. The song tells the story of Molly, who used to sell fish and mussels as she sang, but one day caught a fever and died.

The song goes:

In Dublin's fair city,
Where the girls are so pretty,
I first set my eyes on sweet Molly Malone,
As she wheeled her wheelbarrow,
Through streets broad and narrow,
Crying, "Cockles and mussels, alive, alive, oh!"
She was a fishmonger,
But sure 'twas no wonder,
For so were her father and mother before,
And they each wheeled their barrows,
Through streets broad and narrow,
Crying, "Cockles and mussels, alive, alive, oh!"
She died of a fever,
And no one could save her,
And that was the end of sweet Molly Malone.
But her ghost wheels her barrow,
Through streets broad and narrow,
Crying, "Cockles and mussels, alive, alive, oh!"

Edna sang it with feeling and tears almost poured from her eyes, but I put an end to her crying when I started singing the Fairuz song "Where are they?" which her friend Patrick admired. Then he said, "Tell me about Islam and Libya." Edna interrupted him and warned him, "We didn't come here to talk about religions. Religion is in heaven, or on earth, I don't know."

On the way Patrick went ahead of us and Edna walked by my side. The yellow light of the street lamps cut through the mist and was reflected on the shiny asphalt. The trees on the sides stood firm, defying the wind. The houses were dark except for some faint lighting. It was so quiet that there didn't seem to be anyone in the world but the three of us and our footsteps. Edna said, "Look, that's my star. It always goes with me, alone among the stars, maybe because it's brighter than the others."

"That's why it's alone," I said. "Because it's selfish and can't include the others."

"I'm alone, but I'm not selfish," she said.

"Do you believe in God?" I asked.

She wasn't surprised by the question, because she was drunk and happy. "I don't," she said. "The scandals about priests have made a mockery of religion. People like to live without restrictions. Some of the priests in Ireland have done scandalous things: embezzlement, sexual abuse, incest. I studied religion in the orphanage where I grew up, and when I left at the age of fifteen, I closed the door behind me and left religion in the orphanage."

"The fact that the institution is corrupt doesn't mean the dogma is false," I said. "If the priests lose their way, or the sheikhs in Islam, or the rabbis in Judaism, that doesn't mean that the beliefs are dead or are flawed. The religious theory can be renewed and can still be applied. Being human is the solution."

"You're a philosopher making things complicated," she retorted angrily. "Your Lord is in Cairo. You're a Muslim. But me, I'm happy to live this way. We're here in Ireland." While she put the key in the lock on the front door, I decided never to talk to her about these things again.

Hanan

I received a letter from Cairo in a pink envelope perfumed with Ultraviolet and with drawings of jasmine flowers in the margins. I knew it was from Hanan because she used that fragrance and she had given me some aftershave and shaving lotion of the same brand.

> Moataz,
>
> Cairo is empty and loneliness is a frightening world. Without you I don't do great things. I've stopped studying and I haven't been to any archeological sites since you left Cairo. We often speak about you, Afaf and I. I sent you a card. Did it arrive?

I'm trying to write some poetry, but I can't finish a single verse and most of it is on one subject—loss. I now admit that I miss you and long for you very much. I feel I can't quite breathe, as if I'm in the mountains.

You'd be surprised how I obtained your address. I went to the university and a lecturer who's a friend of yours gave me the address. I was embarrassed but I claimed that I was a relative of yours and had lost touch with you. A white lie that I hope you'll forgive of me.

When are you coming back? I need you. I don't know why but the sense that I need you has grown since you left, and I often cry these days and have bouts of sadness. I often dream that we are together, and you always come to me in my dreams with wings and wearing white. I hope my dreams don't bother you. I'm just anxious about you. I know you're on an important assignment and I'm always proud of you. If you want anything, just send me a letter. How should I end my letter?

I'll say that I'm always waiting for you, so come back safely and don't forget us.

Hanan

Chapter 17

I consumed all my energy moving from one library to another. The university had several reading libraries: the Lecky, the Berkeley, and the library for rare books. I usually sat in the Lecky because it was close to the department where I was studying, so I could have a drink in the cafeteria in the building and chat with the students and faculty, then go to the theater to see some plays or rehearsals.

Sometimes I would go to Eason's bookshop, which lies on the Northside, to buy some books. It was always crowded with visitors. Like paradise, it had several doors and many people would stand at the gates because it was close to McDonald's, the Clarks shoe shop, and Marks and Spencer's.

The old Irishman who sells newspapers outside the bookshop told me that no one asked him for Arabic newspapers except the Algerians because they have problems back home, but he didn't know what they were fighting about. He added automatically, "Islam is the cause of all the trouble in the world." Then, handing me a copy of *al-Ahram*, he said, "Now I prefer Buddhism, because that's the religion that doesn't believe in killing." I didn't respond.

Simone once told me, "The Irish are good people who have suffered greatly from poverty, oppression, disease, and years of trouble with the English. The English took everything, even our self-confidence.

We still depend on them and will continue to do so. Even their language has become our language. And the world looks on and doesn't do anything. Joining the European Union has been a curse, not a blessing, a bribe so that we shut up and join a wide world where our rights and our sacred struggle are ignored, and we grow poorer."

I don't know why Palestine came to my mind, as if it spoke for all those in the world who are oppressed by tyrannical forces.

She added, "Many of us have trouble reading *The Evening Herald* or *The Irish Times*." Then she whispered, "I think the Irish would kill me now if they heard me say that. They don't like anyone to criticize them. They criticize themselves but none of them likes the truth, and this is a problem."

Yes, there's some truth in what Simone says. You have to just listen to them, praise them, and applaud their patriotism. She always says that the Irish are kind, emotional, and generous.

Whenever I went past the George bar, I had a sense of horror and dread. I would quickly cross the road to the other side. When I got off the bus to go to university, I would see it—the only bar that I didn't go near and where I didn't try to look at the customers. Because these men wore strange clothes, and although they looked at me and smiled, I didn't smile back, but looked down at the ground and strode on to the university.

Simone would often take me to bars to listen to Irish folk music. I felt it was monotonous and boring, very much like the raï music of the Maghreb countries. The words and the flute echoed the sadness the two peoples had gone through. We would often go to a bar called the Zanzibar on the northern bank of the Liffey. In the middle of it there were palm trees and a fountain. It was spacious, designed on the inside to look like an Arab or Turkish building. She would be surrounded by friends, but she would always lavish care and love on me. Sometimes I would leave them and go off alone and sit next to the River Liffey at night and listen to its secret murmurings.

Abu Alam put some Knorr potato powder in an aluminum pot half full of water and turned on the electric stove. Then he said, "Five minutes and the soup will be ready."

"I know you're hungry," he said. "The weather here makes you hungry quickly."

"Indeed, but the food here is so bad it doesn't encourage one to eat."

"Who cooks for you?" he asked me.

"I do, sometimes, but the woman I live with doesn't let me cook after eight o'clock in the evening, because once I almost started a fire, so most of my meals are now ready meals. I'm fed up with living here."

"The Irish are said to be generous."

"Sometimes, but only in bars and pubs. They don't invite you home for meals, except at Easter. But in bars they are very generous."

"Is she generous with you?"

"She gives me any cabbage soup that's left over."

He poured the soup into a bowl and said, "There you are."

A modest room in a narrow lane that was paved and clean. Next to the window he had put a plastic pot with some irises in it.

A studio room with a bed, a bathroom, a kitchen, and a small cassette player. I liked the cassette player. I picked it up.

"Nice cassette player. Where did you buy it?"

"I didn't buy it. The girl gave it to me."

"What girl?"

"My sweetheart," he said.

"Algerian?"

"No, Irish."

"And where is she?"

"She left me." He looked sad.

There was a silence and then he started to talk. "She told me, 'We have to break up.' I had had the most beautiful year of my life with her. She was like a dream. She gave me everything, and I gave her my all too. This room and this little, modest bed saw the longest and hottest nights of passion and love. With her lips she kissed every pore in my body." He had the body of a Bohemian artist. He was tall and thin, but well-proportioned, especially in the size of his shoulders and the shape of his legs. His head was beautiful, with a wide forehead and dark eyes that filled half his face, a hooked nose, thin lips with a bluish tinge, and long fingers with prominent veins. He looked like Tutankhamun.

He blew out the smoke of the cigarette he had just lit and looked at the ash that had fallen on his leg. "She took possession of me," he said.

"Try to forget her," I said, coldly and without feeling.

"It's not easy. Haven't you experienced love?"

I didn't answer.

Then he said, "In the beginning I was evasive with her but she ensnared me by giving me everything—money, somewhere to live, love. I'm a Berber and I came to Ireland to avoid the violence in Algeria. I miraculously escaped a massacre in my village in the mountains. I was smuggled out by a Tuareg man along a rugged road through the mountains until I reached the Strait of Gibraltar. Then I slipped into a port and a sailor took me with him after I promised him some money. On the boat, when the captain caught me, I threatened to kill him if he betrayed me to the authorities. I came from Belfast to Dublin. Then I met Sinead in a pub. She invited me to her house and introduced me to her mother, who commented on her daughter's behavior by saying that since she was a child her hobby had been collecting strange things, whatever the cost. In a moment of drunkenness the mother warned me that her daughter was mad and extremely possessive. She said, 'This is dangerous. When it affects women it makes them unable to stick to one man.' I was amazed how a mother could be so critical of her daughter!" He put his cigarette out in a teacup and continued, "Imagine, because I'm a man from the East, I wouldn't make love to her at her house. She used to come late at night and lie with me under the warm bedding, hug me tight, and say, 'Hide me in your arms, ward off the thoughts that trouble my soul, because I am burdened and lost.' While she was in my arms, I said to her, 'I can't live in sin. I'm fed up with illicit sex. Let's get married.'

"She jumped up as if she'd had an electric shock, with her body all trembling. She looked at me in pain and with hostility and mumbled some words that my English wasn't good enough to make out

84

or understand. Then she got dressed, pulled her skirt down over her legs, and squeezed her breasts into a tight blouse, though they still spilled out as if they were angry with me too.

"After some time she changed. She refused to get married, arguing that Arab men treated women as objects and that I would be able to marry another woman, even two or three or four. 'Who told you that?' I asked. She said, 'In Saudi Arabia women walk behind men and cover their bodies and their whole faces. That's unfair. If you want my body, then no marriage. My soul too comes without marriage.' I said 'It's better and purer to do things the proper way.' 'I don't understand much of what you say,' she said."

Then he went to the window and took hold of an iris.

"Forget her," I said.

"I can't," he said in despair. "I'm obsessed with her."

"If you're really religious, why did you agree to sleep with her in the first place?" I asked.

"Western women experiment with making love with a man before marriage. That's their custom when it comes to love and sex," he said.

"But where do the man's wishes come in?" I said, "and who sets the conditions in this relationship? You or her?"

"I was alone and homeless," he said. "And a woman means safety and a sympathetic haven." He stopped a moment, then said with a sigh, "I think her mother was the reason."

"But please, don't think about it too much, you will damage your nerves," I said.

In order to comfort him, I found myself telling him the story of Siham and me, how she made me suffer before I left Cairo, and how my feelings for her grew in exile. I also told him about Simone and how gently she treated me and how she wanted to have a relationship with me. I was relieved to get it off my chest, although he warned me indirectly not to be in a hurry to have a relationship with her, especially when he found out that she was attached to someone else.

I left him and went out into the street, and through the window I caught sight of the iris. He stayed alone thinking of the girl. I asked myself, "Why are you criticizing his relationship with this girl and his obsession with her? You're also involved in your relationship with Siham. You can't run away from her, and you open your arms to her like the dog that was in the cave with the Sleepers of Ephesus, protecting and defending her although she doesn't respond to you in the slightest. You come to your senses too."

The Amr Diab song "Parting is Hell" filled the room, giving me a sense of loneliness and homesickness.

Chapter 18

Bloomsday, June 16

I felt lonely even though the streets were full of people. The sun shone briefly and its rays lit up the horizon. It wasn't very cloudy that day. There were posters everywhere inviting the public to attend poetry sessions, theatrical performances, and readings from James Joyce's *Ulysses*. One announced a trip to the center of Dublin to trace the same streets, the same lanes, and the same bars and shops that Bloom, the hero of the novel, visited on that day more than ninety years earlier. I went to the university and photocopied some material, and while I was coming out I saw a young man reading a novel by Naguib Mahfouz. When I asked him what nationality he was, he said he was American. He said that he very much liked Mahfouz because he represented the civilized aspect of the Arabs, because his philosophical way of thinking showed that Egyptians had scientific minds. He continued that the philosophical knowledge he reflects in his novels and in the logic of his main characters proves rather than disproves that God exists, as claimed by those who accuse him of atheism. I said, "Are they interested in Arabs in America?" The United States was attacking Sudan at the time and this affected the rapport between us, although he did invite me to have a cup of coffee with him in Bewley's. "Have you read Joyce too?" I asked him. "I'm trying," he said, "and I don't understand him. I think the Irish themselves don't understand him. We have a custom in the United States now that your bookcase should have a copy of *Ulysses* so that you can pretend to people that you're cultured." I said, "Naguib Mahfouz and Joyce have some features in common. They were both interested in questions of the nation. Mahfouz admitted that he read Joyce when he was working in the Ministry of Religious Endowments library. Kamal Abdel Gawad, the hero of the trilogy, and Stephen Dedalus in *Ulysses* have the same concerns: man and his destiny. Even the narrative space and place in *Ulysses* and in Mahfouz are similar: Dublin at the beginning of the twentieth century and Gamaliya, and also the rulers and the revolutionaries—de Valera, Michael Collins, and Parnell here, Mustafa Kamel, Saad Zaghloul, and the Wafdists in Egypt—and their desire for liberation from British imperialism."

I wondered, "What is America? Is it a friend or an enemy? Is it a beacon of freedom and the apostle of democracy, or is it the Great Satan, as Khomeini says? Is America justice, freedom, and equality, or is it *Star Wars* and *The Silence of the Lambs*? Is it the American Dream and progress, or tyranny and hegemony? Is it Christianity with its tolerance, forgiveness, and charity, or is it the Crusades, Zionism, Freemasonry, and ambitions in the East? Is it the ally of good or of evil?" I was hesitant to answer these questions, which ran riot in my head.

I left the university and crossed the road to the beginning of Grafton Street. There were some young women playing a piece by Mozart. All I could do was stand there, riveted to the spot, ravished by the wonderful melody.

Close by there was an artist drawing on the roadway the scene of Ophelia drowning in the brook, surrounded by daffodils everywhere. There was a look in her eyes that conveyed a combination of surprise, sadness, and grief, but it was very far from mad. I don't know why I stayed to look so long, although I had walked past this impromptu artist many times when I came out of the university and I had waited next to him at the bus stop. But this time the picture pulled me in, as if I were looking into a deep grave full of existential secrets. I grieved for the fate that awaited Ophelia,

Hamlet's wretched admirer. I had images of Siham and the fate of our relationship: a big theatrical act, and madness was our probable destiny.

I walked around Temple Bar. I met Simone and she invited me to attend a reading of some new Irish novels in celebration of Bloomsday, the day when Bloom, the hero of *Ulysses*, went out to see Dublin: June 16, 1904, the same day Joyce met his future wife Nora, and the same day that Bloom left his house at 7 Eccles Street. Most of the novelists had come from the United States for this event. I didn't feel that they were Irish, and neither did Simone, who commented, "Why do they come to us? And what do they know about our society? All they do is sell our history and our lives to Irish emigrants. They collect money there, then come here to collect memories and write about us as if we are mythical creatures fit only for literary folklore."

I was happy listening to these writers. One of them, Edna O'Brien, had written a biography of Joyce. But at the same time, I began to feel uncomfortable and tense, and I asked myself, "Am I a novelist? Am I a writer? Will I become famous some day?"

Chapter 19

Edna's daughter Britney was always silent. She didn't talk to me at all. She was only interested in her dog Fraser. I asked Edna if she could take the dog out to the garden, where it had its own kennel, or at least give it a bath. Mark shared my opinion and told me he had argued with her several times over the dog. I explained to him why I didn't like dogs. I said Muslims think that dog saliva is unclean and if a dog licks its owner's hand or puts its mouth into a jug or a pot then the thing will be unclean for forty days. If we want to get rid of the impurity, then it has to be done with soil or through a complete ritual bath. But I also told him there was nothing wrong with using guard dogs. "That's unfair," he said, "though I agree with you that the saliva is harmful." Then he announced, "Muslims are cruel." I was stunned. But I told him several sayings of the Prophet Muhammad that urge Muslims to be kind to animals.

"One woman went to Hell because she locked up a cat," I said. "Then there was the man who went down a well and had a drink, then he cupped his hands to give water to a thirsty dog, and he went to Heaven."

But Mark wasn't convinced.

Mark loved Britney. He was always buying her gifts and giving her cards. "She lives like an orphan," he said. "She's like the daughter I haven't had and never will, because I'm old now and no woman would put up with me. Who would put up with a poor old man like me? It's my fate to be single and I might die alone in my room when Edna's away. I'd lie dead in my room and the only thing that would show I was dead would be that dog, because it would be able to see my soul as it left my body, and it would mourn me by barking and Britney would be very sad to lose me. That's why I like them—because they'll show respect when I die, like family."

Britney's hobby was sculpture, especially making statues of horses, and she liked to watch horse races on television. She sat for hours in front of the television recording the races. In my room alone there were three different models of horses, and in her room, which I never entered, there were sixty horses, according to her mother. I caught sight of them when I went down the stairs near her room. She was also vegetarian. She would put her rice and vegetables in the microwave, then take her plate, sit in the living-room and watch television, or go up to her room. She didn't speak to anyone either, especially me. It was like I wasn't there with her. Sometimes we exchanged a few short sentences when her mother or Mark were there. Britney was longing to go to Germany and work. Her sister had invited her there.

Britney was an introvert. She didn't like to talk to strangers, but Edna assured me that as the days passed she would get used to me.

Then, enthusiastically and with a touch of sadness, she added that Britney had been like that since childhood. She suffered from autism. I think that losing her father when she was young was the reason for what happened to her. I tried to guess why she preferred horses to all other animals and why she kept the dog in her room despite the awful smell.

Edna said, "My daughter is frightened of foreigners, like most Irish people, because we were isolated for a long time. We didn't know anything about the outside world. The English and the Scots visit us on weekends by ferry." Then she added contemptuously, "They spend their money on board before they land at Dun Laoghaire, and they take the opportunity to flirt with the Irish women." Then, in pain and sorrow, she said, "Some Irish men don't like the English, and they don't appreciate the Scots either despite the ties of blood. Now foreigners from all over come to Ireland. The country has set up relations with all the countries in Europe and the rest of the world, but at this stage they're not prepared for such a foreign presence. They're worried their country will be occupied, as it was by the English in the past. I think that in ten years' time you won't find this problem. Everything will change if only we're a little patient."

Chapter 20

How Eve feels after tasting the fruit of the tree of Knowledge of Good and Evil:

> But I feel
> Farr otherwise th' event, not Death, but Life
> Augmented, op'nd Eyes, new Hopes, new Joyes,
> Taste so Divine, that what of sweet before
> Hath toucht my sense, flat seems to this, and harsh.
> On my experience, ADAM, freely taste,
> And fear of Death deliver to the Windes.
> Milton, Paradise Lost

When Simone invited me to her house for dinner, I thought she would be alone, but I found her house crowded with guests. As usual, she welcomed me warmly and introduced me graciously to her friends. Then we had dinner and we all sat down and she began to play the piano, and then her sister accompanied her on the fiddle. A friend of hers sang along with them, and when she had finished she asked me to sing them an Egyptian song. I sang and received some applause. Then we had a break from music and we all went back to our seats. A young man came up to me, and when she noticed him, Simone approached too and introduced me to him. It was Brendan, the boyfriend she had often spoke about. He looked me over, then praised my voice and asked me about the song. I told him it was an Abdel Halim Hafez song called "Day has passed" and I explained to him what the words meant, since he had asked.

He said, "Do you like Egypt after what it's done to its neighbors?"

"Who do you mean, its neighbors?" I asked.

"Palestine. Egypt sold out the Palestinian cause to serve its own interests." Then he talked about America's relationship with the Middle East and how Egypt had allowed America to attack Iraq in 1991. I felt insulted when Brendan attacked Egypt's policy on Palestine, saying it had kowtowed to Israel and America and strengthened the West's presence since the peace treaty with Israel. "Why does everyone here talk about that treaty?" I wondered. But I couldn't win him over to my point of view, which was that if it hadn't been for the treaty, Sinai would not have been recovered, which was what I had learned in history books at school. I hadn't asked myself how useful it was or what purpose it served. I remembered what my Nasserist friend used to say when he criticized Sadat in the debates at the Tagammu Party. I didn't agree with much of what he said because he was unfair to Sadat on many occasions. He thought that the treaty had left a legacy of capitulation and held back the development of Sinai. It had turned it into an area where there were no Egyptians, no serious investment, and not even an army to protect it, other than in some tourist resorts and beaches for Israelis and Russians, and that it had turned Egyptians into servants for those who came only for pleasure. He said that the treaty meant that most of the crossing points were closed to defenseless Palestinians, who were suffering and expiring on the borders and the crossing points to Gaza and Rafah. The treaty meant land in exchange for peace. Yes, there is peace, but there are also Egyptians who have to undergo identity checks to cross Sinai, as if they were strangers in their own land, though thousands of people gave their lives to win it back.

Israel has built settlements for Jewish immigrants on about two-thirds of the West Bank and has developed the occupied territories to a much greater extent than Egypt has built up Sinai for Egyptians, who are clustered in slums without basic services, and are deprived of decent housing unless they have thousands of pounds to pay for a small apartment of no more than sixty square meters.

The treaty was a golden opportunity to ensure Israel's survival and to keep the Arabs and the Egyptians weak. Yes, we have to preserve the peace but on condition of strength, justice, every party's legitimate right to exist, and development for Egyptians and Palestinians. Yes, we have big internal problems such as unemployment and bureaucracy, which make you uninterested in the political role that the state plays abroad, but what I have come to realize is that the state has become poor in spite of development attempts and is unable to satisfy many of the people.

Then I said to Brendan, "Peace is the only option, and perhaps making peace was submission to the will of the United States, but on the other hand, violence has not helped end the suffering of the people of Palestine and Syria."

He said, "Resistance is the answer. It's legitimate to resist to obtain territory and freedom."

Suddenly I said, "Ireland has been trying to liberate itself by violence for four centuries, and all the conspiracies and conferences that Gerry Adams organizes will not solve the problem. America and England have their own agreement on the future of this artistic people, who love stout and singing more than they love weapons and violence."

He said, "Your experience of life in Ireland comes from bars and quiet streets. Give yourself a chance to discover the revolutionary side of it, but don't treat reality from a dreamy, romantic point of view, or else you won't live long. You'll lose a lot." What does he mean by saying "You won't live long"? Is he planning something? Maybe he's referring to something to do with my relationship with Simone. She herself admitted she had spoken to him about how she likes me. So why is he trying to be objective with me? Did Simone tell him to treat me politely, especially as I was her guest? Why didn't he bring up the question of my relationship with Simone? Was he putting that off? Did he want to get his revenge suddenly without anyone noticing, as Abu Alam had said? Would he wait for me in some dark corner and stab me as soon as I came out of Simone's house, or would he put poison in my tea? Was his love for Simone over? Did he welcome her having a new lover? Or was it that he didn't feel that there was any danger from me and it didn't mean anything to him now?

Simone noticed that I was tense, so she said, "Let's sing again!" Then she sang the Sinead O'Connor song "Nothing compares 2 u," and Brendan joined us in the song. He was staring at Simone and his singing was addressed to her.

After a time the party broke up, and to my surprise, Brendan left the house completely drunk, leaning on the shoulder of one of the women. He was looking at me angrily and I wanted to leave but Simone asked me to stay. Perhaps she was afraid Brendan would lie in wait to attack me, so I deferred to her wishes. She said, "You can sleep here tonight," but I was reluctant.

Chapter 21

She pulled me forcefully toward her and pressed her warm hands into my backbone and ribs. "Don't get up," she said. "I want you to stay longer."

She kissed me close to my ear. Then she pressed her mouth to my neck. I felt the wetness of her saliva, hot and moist, and we ended up kissing deeply.

The candles burning in the room gave me a sense of seclusion and primitiveness. Although the weather was cold outside, I was sweating. When I tried to get up, she pulled me by my hand and her pudgy fingers touched my fingertips. She went to the drawer and pulled out a towel with a strong smell that reeked of sweat and the body fluids associated with making love.

"Please don't leave now," she said.

"Let me go," I said. "I can't stay here." Then I headed for the door.

"Don't go," she said. "I want you beside me. Stay with me. I'm sorry. I know you don't want to go on with this relationship until I end my relationship with Brendan. Then we would get married, or perhaps there's another woman in your life.

"Stay," she whispered. "We can talk about it later."

"I want to leave now. I feel like I'm suffocating," I said.

She threw herself onto the edge of the bed and started to cry. I looked at her and the tears flowed from her eyes. Then she rose, adjusting her hair, which hung down over her wet forehead. "You can go now. Do what you want," she shouted.

I read:

> Quiet then muteness then silence
> Knowledge then ecstasy then tomb
> Clay then fire then light
> Cold then shadow then sun
> Sorrow then ease then wasteland
> River then ocean then dryness
> Drunkenness then sobriety then longing
> Nearness then juncture then intimacy
> Contraction then expansion then effacement
> Separation then meeting then annihilation
> Expressions used by people for whom
> This world is worth just a penny
> There are voices behind the door but
> Close up the expressions people use are whispers
>   Al-Hallaj, *Clay and Fire*

Everything is permissible here. No relatives, no brothers, no appearances to keep up, so I can do anything. My body aches with desires and the need to be included, while my mind restrains my body's wild impulses. My body is hungry to embrace and let go.

It's hard for people to include you here because they all go their own way, it's hard to explain what you want, and if you get involved in something you have to carry it though to the end. Freedom is relative and conventions don't lapse with a change of country, but inside me they tie me down and incapacitate me. I want and long to make love to a woman, even if I don't love her, even if it's Simone.

My body is heavy, and I feel like I'm carrying it on my shoulders.

I have to work. I don't have any money. I'll rely on myself and I won't write to my mother asking her for money, although when I speak to her on the phone, she says, "Ask for whatever you want and I'll send it to you."

I could sell newspapers or flowers. Many young people do casual work. I'd rather not work in a bar or a pub. I'm deterred by a long religious and psychological history. God cursed alcohol and those who carry it or serve it or drink it, and so on till the end of the saying of the Prophet. And besides, no good can come of money earned though work that's haram. I carry with me a heritage of puritanism and paternalism.

My Italian friend Mario, who I met at university and who's studying art, said, "If you don't have any money, you should ask for welfare from the Irish government. They provide money to foreigners."

"And what do I do to get that welfare?"

"Just go to the immigration department and present yourself as a political refugee."

"But I'm not a political refugee. I'm here to work on my doctorate!"

"I know all that, but this is the way you can get some money."

I said, "I don't want to put myself in an embarrassing situation. I'm not a political refugee and I don't want to haggle over anything. And besides, my country hasn't done me any harm. It hasn't persecuted me. On the contrary, I feel at peace in Cairo whereas here I feel homesick and in need. Here I'm nothing. There's no market here for my learning or for people to teach English literature." I quoted the folk proverb: "I've come to sell water in the lane where the water carriers live." Is what I'm saying true? Hasn't my country persecuted me by neglecting me, ignoring my suffering, and treating me as insignificant?

He seemed to have read my mind. "My friend, don't be idealistic or chauvinistic. All foreigners do that, and more. Some of them claim they've suffered religious or sexual persecution in their countries and claim that they're seeking freedom in a country where the individual isn't sent to prison just because they differ in their beliefs or sexual orientation, and Ireland doesn't pay a penny from its own pocket, but it comes from a United Nations refugee budget.

"Think of yourself and don't be embarrassed. All of us do that. I'm here avoiding military service. For me, Ireland is involuntary exile. There were two options: either doing military service for a year or studying in another European country for the same period, so I chose to study, not because I like it, but to avoid bigger issues. We young people don't have a role to play now, except for having sex and working hard to make money. These are the new ideologies and the new world order. Don't believe in anything except saving enough money to buy what's on the market. People are the last thing to believe in. Being a citizen now means having a bank balance, and a nation means a house somewhere in the world where you can take refuge when you need to."

As if addressing myself, I said that even sex isn't allowed in Egypt, let alone money. I put myself in this position and no one forced me into it. I chose to study away from home and to take responsibility for covering the cost of my studies. I sometimes wonder who would really be interested in helping me. And who's interested in my country? What am I doing here? I'm ignored here and at a loss there. Who cares that I suffer for the sake of knowledge? Has the university ever thought of sending me a letter asking me how much money and support I need?

The pounds I earned teaching Arabic and English to foreigners were not enough to live in Dublin. I gave English lessons to a young Italian called Antonio who was good-looking and strongly built, though he did have a slipped disc. Most of the time I gave him lessons as he lay on his back. After a month of teaching, he told me that I brought him good luck because God in His good grace had cured him, and he vowed that whenever I visited him in his house he would cook pasta for me. I tasted every kind of Italian pasta and tried every kind of sauce that any Italian could ever dream up, such as mushroom sauce, garlic, tomato, cheese, chicken sauce, minced beef, and also vegetable. He was kind and worked all night looking after old and retired people, giving them medicine, reading to them, and helping them go to the bathroom and wash themselves.

I also taught Arabic to a young Frenchman called Lusini. After a few sessions I discovered that he was Jewish and he was learning Arabic because he wanted to study Middle East politics. Once he admitted he had Egyptian roots and his grandfather left Egypt after the war of 1948 and migrated to Israel, then went to England and settled there. He was surprised to discover that for a long time Ireland didn't have a single synagogue and that it was the only European country that Jews didn't go to. I remembered what Mr. Deasy said in *Ulysses*, that Ireland had the honor of being the only country which never persecuted the Jews "because she never let them in."

I don't know why, but after that I stopped going to give him Arabic lessons, despite his polite manner and his progress in studying the language, and on top of that his lack of racism or Zionism.

I also worked in an Indian restaurant called Kandahar in Harold's Cross, from four o'clock to half past midnight. I mopped the restaurant floor, carried sacks of onions into the kitchen and peeled them, and broke up heads of garlic. After that I washed the dishes and cooked the rice and the chef taught me how to cook Chinese boiled rice and basmati rice with spices.

There was a Pakistani man working with me in the restaurant, but he was weird and often gave me odd looks and spoke with amazement about how my skin was so white. Several times he invited me to the home of the restaurant owner where young men from all the Indian- and Pakistani-owned restaurants in Ireland met. I went with them to the house, which had several floors. On each floor, there were multiple rooms in which young men in the prime of life lived. They played backgammon and cards and the young men were not allowed to sit with the older ones or play games with them. I was tense when I went into the place and I asked, "Aren't there any women in this house?"

"The women are in another house," the Pakistani man said.

In one room, which was full of smoke and the smell of opium and marijuana, there was a group of young men dancing to Indian music. The others were lying on cushions cuddling each other. I was taken aback and frightened, and I asked my friend if I could leave. He was surprised.

"I thought you'd feel at home in this atmosphere," he said.

"You misunderstood," I said. "This isn't my lifestyle."

Then a young woman came in wearing a veil with a teapot in her hand, and poured us cups of tea mixed with basil and cloves.

Some of the young men asked her to dance with them, and she took off her veil and started to dance. Her body was swinging and swaying with extraordinary agility. She had a supple waist, she was excited by the music and she was jumping nimbly from place to place. Then she went to the restaurant owner and leaned over him. He kissed her on the mouth and cheek and she let her hair hang over him. He took her in his arms, gave her a deep kiss and took her off to a secluded corner of the room. I wanted to leave, so the restaurant owner asked my friend to drive me home, and he agreed.

I rushed down the stairs to escape this Kandahari experience.

You will come to greatly regret that you didn't get to know these people better and that you didn't listen to their stories and find out why these Afghans, Kurds, and Pakistanis live dispersed around the world. The whole world will go to them and try to find out more about them and who they are, whether by writing books about them or with rockets and rifles. September 11 was a decisive day in the history of Muslim nations and in the history of America. The whole world will go there, not just to fight al-Qaeda, to trace the footsteps of Bin Laden, and to find out how many exits and entrances there are to the caves where the al-Qaeda mujahideen and the Afghans hide, but to discover oil wells and to collect cannabis and poppies, because the opium of Afghanistan has more strategic importance than mountains and deep oil wells.

The United States will draw a new map of Asia and of the world by controlling this rugged patch of the world. That day will become a black spot in the history of America. The desire to take revenge on al-Qaeda, even if the organization wasn't the perpetrator as skeptics say, will become the supreme objective of the U.S. government, if not of the world that rejects violent resistance. The ideologue of the attacks on the Twin Towers will continue to overshadow the corpses of the bearded men, the women, children, and old men in the mountains and on the plains of Afghanistan and Pakistan, and the specter of Bin Laden will continue to haunt the world, and is bound always to come to you in your dreams in the form of a bearded man wearing bedouin clothes, standing there next to the Kaaba giving the pilgrims wine and blood to drink.

Hanan's letter was a wake-up call for my emotions. So she missed me and maybe she loved me. She knew that I loved Siham. It's true I hadn't told her but everyone close to us knew what had happened between us, and Afaf would volunteer to tell my story. Hanan was an innocent in a tarnished and corrupted world. Her emotions had a freshness that contrasted with the jaded, rigid scene around her. Where is she? And where am I? I'm alone here living drunken nights without touching a drop and drowning in guilt without committing any sins. My big concern is Siham, but my reality now is Simone, because I've started thinking about Simone, about the state she's in and what will become of me with her because she's determined we should be together and live in the same apartment after she's sorted things out with her boyfriend. But I found out that she was lying to me and that she was still meeting him. That's what her English friend Sari told me secretly. She said I wouldn't be able to get out of it because her boyfriend was very angry and hated the fact that I knew her, and she was afraid he might do me harm if my relationship with her continued. Simone had grown closer to me and was playing the role of my patron. She had started bringing me books that might help me in my research and was booking theater tickets for me. She was trying to draw my attention to cultural and political events taking place in Dublin, was showing respect for my private rituals and for my conservatism as a Muslim man, and was admitting that to satisfy her as a woman it was enough for me just to look at her or touch her fingertips.

I was delighted with this interest, because it was new to have a woman so strongly attached to me. It was a real test of my masculinity and of my desire to put an end to my virginity, which had almost reached the level of monasticism and which might in the end have made me lose my enthusiasm for women and maybe for femininity, but my doubts began to grow when her friend Sari spoke to me about her ex-boyfriend's desire to take revenge on me. I started to get really paranoid when I thought I saw men watching me at night, or when some of the young people in the area where I lived made pointless attempts to harass me verbally and physically, especially as I was coming back from her place. I told Abu Alam of my fears, and he corroborated them and advised me to be careful, because I might end up drowned in a pool of mud after they stripped me and tarred and feathered me to humiliate me.

I thought that someone who kills in the name of his country might kill someone who steals his girlfriend. Why not? Hasn't land been analogous to women throughout the ages? Adam lost Paradise and gained another paradise and another land—Eve.

So I tried to keep away from Simone and I avoided the places where we might meet. I would stay in the library for long periods and I wouldn't answer the telephone because I knew it was she who was always calling me. Was I such a coward? Was I so paranoid about what this English woman said that I hid from Simone? I knew that Sari didn't like Simone and wanted her to leave the group so that she could take it over for herself, and Simone also hated Sari and, in an exaggerated manner, saw her as a symbol of English colonialism in Dublin because of her arrogance and obstinacy. But I decided to be brave and tell Simone of my fears and what I was thinking. I didn't love her sincerely, and perhaps that way I could break free and she would set me free.

Chapter 22

One night I ran out of money. It was a cold night and the frost had made my limbs stiff. It began to rain and I missed the eleven-thirty bus, which was the last bus. I had no money with me.

I stood in Dame Street, after one o'clock at night, begging for money.

"Sir, do you have twenty-five pence?"

To my surprise someone gave me fifty pence.

Moataz. What are you doing? Are you begging? What if your friends saw you? What if your head of department saw you? I would say that the public transport had stopped and I didn't have enough money for a taxi. I didn't want to stop a taxi driver and beg him to take me home for free. Yes, some of these taxi drivers are kind and would see the shame of poverty in my eyes and agree to give me a lift.

I came to my senses when a hand put some coins in my hand. The Irish are charitable. They took pity on me and gave away whatever they had at hand. Their kindness wiped out all the effects of the anger and irritation that I sometimes felt because of the behavior of a few idiots. I collected a fair amount of money. At the side of the road there was a bunch of flowers that had been thrown next to a trash can. I went up to them, an idea took shape in my head, and I decided to sell the flowers instead of begging. I remembered how I used to sell flowers when I was a student in

Cairo, and how I saved some of the money to cover some of my university expenses.

I picked up the bouquet and offered it to passers-by. Some of the men welcomed the chance to buy a flower to show their love for their sweethearts, and were willing to pay handsomely, while others said the woman they were with was their sister or their wife, so they didn't need flowers. So here was a job, a freelance job that wouldn't disrupt my studies and didn't require a work permit, because I was in Dublin only to study and the authorities wouldn't have agreed to give me such a permit. I remembered the flower seller and I decided to go and see her and get some flowers I could sell at night in Temple Bar.

Abu Alam told me: "These Irish are very kind."

"Not very!" I replied.

"Fairly kind, but the Church corrupted them and they lost their way. This country needs reform. Islam would be a great solution for it. They are generous by nature. I believe that if they converted to Islam it would be very good for them."

"You're talking like the people I've run away from. Tell me, what's going on in your head?" I said.

"No, nothing," he said. "I don't mean conversion by violence. What's happening in Algeria has nothing to do with religion. It's a struggle between the interests of one faction and another faction.

"The Islamic Salvation Front and the government each want to achieve some purpose. The government provoked the front by ignoring the Islamists and writing them out of politics after their overwhelming victory in the elections in the early 1990s. Violence broke out and close to one hundred and fifty thousand innocent people died in this conflict. Religion has intervened in politics, but I want peace to come about."

"Do you think religion is the answer?" I asked him.

He looked distracted, then replied, "I was joking. There's no need to think too much about what I said. I want to feel happy and at peace in any way possible."

Then he asked me, "Moataz, do you believe? Do you perform your religious obligations as you should?"

I couldn't come up with an answer.

I asked myself, "Do you really believe?"

"I'm peaceable by nature. I don't offend anyone. I don't deny anyone their rights without good reason. I don't lie. I study hard. I'm sympathetic toward others. I love children and respect my elders. I avoid sin whenever I can but sometimes I slip up and then I say I'll be perfect one day and I ask for forgiveness."

"Have the extreme levels of materialism around us killed our souls?" he asked.

"I don't deny that studying English literature and philosophy has developed my ability to use reason: to be inquisitive and ask questions in spite of everything. I don't even take metaphysical things for granted. I examine them and analyze them. Don't I have a right to do that? The patriarch Abraham was uncertain until he found God. He looked at the sun and the moon, and in the end he arrived at the truth."

"But the situation is different now," Abu Alam said with a smile. "Abraham was the ancestor of the prophets, but we're living at the end of the twentieth century, and all the revealed religions exist and have reached maturity, and the three holy books are available everywhere. The message is clear and straightforward, so there's no need to doubt, or search for the truth, or lose ourselves in existential diversions. Islam really could solve many of the troubles of this city."

"You shouldn't say that in public because people are sensitive about religion here," I said. Then I told him about the Irishman I met in a pub who told me threateningly, "I'm going to the South Circular Road to set fire to the Muslims' mosque there. They have destroyed everything. They come here buying up the churches and synagogues and then they turn them into mosques. I'm frightened of Islam. It's the religion of violence and fanaticism. Ireland would be a paradise without religion. Even the Church has less of a grip on us now. The Church is now a McDonald's restaurant. Go to Wicklow and see. We don't want more authorities." I was afraid of him. He was drunk. His girlfriend, who touched my hand flirtatiously from time to time, tried to calm him down. "Don't take any notice," she said.

Then she asked me if I wanted to take her home with me to have a Guinness.

I turned down her invitation because she wasn't pretty. But she did have very distinctive breasts. She wasn't wearing a bra, so she let them move around freely whenever she made a sudden movement and she left her blouse unbuttoned down to her sexy cleavage, where I could see the bones between her loose breasts. I noticed a golden piece of jewelry like my grandmother's necklace, slightly faded. I had suspicions that she was a drug addict after I saw signs of needle-pricks in one of her veins.

Chapter 23

Lilacs and lilies, lilacs and lilies,
Two bunches for four pounds, three for five.

The sellers gathered around the flower cart that was dragged along on rickety wheels, and because they were so well-dressed, I didn't think of them as sellers but as ladies preparing themselves for a romantic evening by arranging flowers. They handed them to customers and looked around anxiously as if they felt they were in imminent danger. When I saw them, they reminded me of my experience selling flowers in Cairo, especially in the nightclubs there. When I was a child I used to sell flowers on Qasr al-Nil bridge and in front of the Semiramis Hotel.

"How much are the roses?"

"Expensive."

"Too expensive for me?"

They looked at me from top to toe from behind the handcart on which they had put their flowers. A customer came forward to buy some flowers. They busied themselves selling to her.

"Do you want to buy or are you just wasting time?"

"But give me a discount. I'm poor."

"You look like a prince. Where are you from? Italian or French?"

"No, I'm Egyptian."

"Allahu Akbar," one of them intoned with a smile.

"Who taught you that phrase?" another one asked.

"We Irish, we know everything," she said.

One of them came up to me flirtatiously, as if she were going to kiss me or embrace me.

"My husband's sister is married to a very rich Saudi who gives her lots of gold to wear," she said.

Suddenly one of the flower sellers panicked, and they started to rush over O'Connell Bridge, which crosses the River Liffey.

"The flowers!" I said.

One of them handed me a bouquet. I gave her five pounds and said, "Tomorrow I'll give you the rest of the money." But suddenly a third woman, who was standing with them, grabbed the bouquet from me. She was short and not as pretty as the others.

"No, we don't know you," she said.

"Give it to him," replied the plump one with the beautiful blonde hair, the bronze complexion, and eyes the color of mountain honey.

Then she took it from the cart, handed it to me, and said, "Come back tomorrow."

I smiled and thanked her.

You're going to sell flowers. This is the easiest and quickest solution. You don't have a job here and you're not allowed to work because you have a student visa. What else can you do?

An extra in a historical film, you're wearing military uniform, with a helmet on your head. You look at the principal actors in awe, enviously, hoping that the director will give you a role in which you have some words to say, or a role as a whore-mongering striptease dancer who stands on a circular stage in the middle of a cheap bar, taking your clothes off one by one until you're completely naked, with nothing to cover your private parts. You twist and turn around a cold metal pole, with the lights and the eyes of the women and men all trained on you! You turn on the floor like a whore and lift your legs like a prostitute with your fingers pointing toward your private parts and the women scream. The men throw banknotes at you and you get excited and jump around like a monkey. The deprived and the perverted desire you, but is your body sexy enough? Do you have strapping muscles, a well-proportioned body, sexy and seductive skin, sparkling eyes, sculpted features, and a Roman or Jewish nose that proves your virility?

So what would you do if you did agree to do a striptease?

You'd go to a photographer who frequents the George bar. He'd ask you to take off your clothes, and you'd smear your body with Vaseline and give him various poses of the kind made by those who make a profession of charm and seduction, and then you'd send your photos to modeling agents to market your body and your private parts.

Is this what you aspired to? Is this what you wanted from your trip, or is this, Moataz, what's going on in your subconscious? How dare you do that! A young man from the East, bearing a dream of learning and knowledge in a Western world that is famous for that, a serious young man from the poor quarters, carrying the wealth of his intellect and an iron will, a young man who grew up in a family of the middling sort, content with the meager pension that the head of the family received after the factory where he worked was privatized. The father struggled to educate his children, convinced by Gamal Abdel Nasser's discourse on the value of education as an engine of social change, and confident that learning, knowledge, and excellence could overcome the stigma of poverty and low birth, because excellence has a price. His father believed what Abdel Nasser said, and remained loyal to that and to the man throughout his life. He convinced Moataz of that despite all the obstacles he faced. He would study and excel and get his doctorate. The son of the pious worker, he would join the elite, just like the children of the nouveau riche or the ruthless people who engaged in corruption. He would prove to everyone that in times of corruption and crisis there are values we have to uphold, that Nasserism will not die, that science is the magic weapon to solve our problems and overcome the inferiority complexes of the human race. A father who has five children. He and his country-born wife do their best to produce useful citizens for an anarchic society. But society no longer recognizes their usefulness. It recognizes other things, but nonetheless the old armies are still deployed, the old promise still stands, despite all the storms and waves that force fathers to trample their children underfoot so that they can escape drowning in corruption.

Chapter 24

Fall came early that year, or so they said. The leaves fell dead on the narrow pathways, and only the Angel of Death knew their number and what type they were. The faces of the passers-by and the students turned white because of the bitter cold. I wrapped myself up in many layers and the coat I had brought with me from Cairo stopped the cold penetrating my bones, which began to ache in a way that was unusual. My friend Mario advised me to drink alcohol—the elixir that would help me acclimatize to Ireland. He said, "If you don't drink alcohol and you don't sleep with women, then what's life for?"

Frida prepared the flowers for me, wrapping them in cellophane and licking the ends with her tongue to make the wrapping stick. "My husband thinks I prefer foreigners to the people of my own country," she said. "He's English and I'm Irish. Yes, he persecutes me but I love him. I've grown addicted to him. He's now an inseparable part of my life. I'm tormented in this life, always wandering the streets, as you can see, pursued by the police because I haven't got a license to sell. I've been like that since I was a child, selling flowers and helping my mother bring up my seven brothers and sisters. We Irish love children. Birth control has no place with us. It's a trick by others to wipe out our people. The famine killed millions, and most of our ancestors emigrated to America. Emigration became second nature to us. The world seemed to be disowning us. Except America. Four of my brothers and sisters moved there." She was interrupted by the voice of a flower seller called Rebecca, who was singing the Céline Dion song "Immortality." The final line "We don't say goodbye" was repeated.

As she sang I remembered Cairo and singing on Qasr al-Nil bridge. Then she blew me a kiss with her sensual lips, and I grabbed it affectionately and shyly. Then she said, "My first husband was a drunk, and he beat me as well: an odious person. Yes, I had a boy and a girl with him, but I'm happy with this Englishman despite everything I suffer. I know he's stealing my money but what can I do?"

I suggested she act tough and not be defeatist, and that she reject this humiliating situation. I told her about my sister, who was faithful to her husband for fourteen years, and then he left her for another woman and took her daughter and her two sons off to Hungary with the woman, who was fifteen years older than him. She fought to get back the girl, whom she hadn't seen for seven years. She was defeatist. Love had taught her self-sacrifice, but her husband read her fidelity as submission and surrender, so he took liberties. Now she's alone, living with her daughter in my mother's house. He doesn't let her see the two boys. I think she's going to lose her mind. She's always arguing with my mother, and she always annoys us with the way she lives. I paused and I said, "Perhaps the reason I'm here is to get away from there. I hate the way she has capitulated—and her face reminds me how humiliating it can be when people are weak."

Frida leaned her torso against the wall along the Liffey and threw up into the river. We gathered around her.

"You should go to a doctor," I said.

"She doesn't need a doctor," said Rebecca. "She needs a midwife, because she's pregnant."

Frida looked at me with worried eyes. Then she said sadly, "Another child that's haram, as your religion puts it." Then suddenly she shouted out hysterically, "Allahu akbar, Allahu akbar."

I took my flowers and went off, leaving behind me the Liffey, scraps of bread, and a bitter taste in my throat, mixed with river water.

Chapter 25

The streets of Dublin are long and narrow. The center of the city is divided into a northern and a southern part, defined by the River Liffey, which runs through the city. There are numerous bridges linking the two halves, including the O'Connell Bridge and the Ha'penny Bridge. The houses are no higher than three or four stories, and the most important feature of them is their beautiful doors. With its houses and its doors, the city looks like a large mural made of colored rectangles. The deeper you go into the southern district, the steeper and more twisty the streets become, and it's hard for someone walking to handle the steep parts unless they have strong knees. The city center is usually crowded, especially at rush hour, like all big capitals, but it calms down on Saturdays and Sundays to become almost deserted. At night, foreigners flock into Temple Bar, in a district in Southside famous for its bars and pubs.

Since Temple Bar is close to the river port, the houses there were used in the eighteenth and nineteenth centuries as inns and hotels for foreigners and travelers, where they could find food and houses of pleasure cheaply. The main square was used for performing religious plays, and Handel put on a performance of his oratorio *Messiah* in a music hall nearby in 1742. Over the next two centuries, the area became neglected. In the twentieth century, certain institutions renovated the area and the Irish Film Institute was set up, showing European and contemporary films. In Temple Bar there is now a theater and center to teach music. In one of the main streets there was a small coffee shop called Deja Vu, which served only Turkish coffee and which stayed open till the morning. It was dark inside, lit only by candles, and in it you could hear jazz and the blues, especially Louis Armstrong and Bessie Smith and her sad song "After you've gone." I would sit there alone, thinking about my life, my studies, and my desire to write a new novel about Siham and my family. It was Simone who showed me the place and explained to me what "déjà vu" meant. I often wished that Siham could be with me. She would definitely have loved the place. Perhaps it could be a theatrical space for one of her novels or stories. The regulars from the George and the surrounding bars always sat there. The Scots and the people from Northern Ireland came to Temple Bar for pleasure and for women. They also came for bachelorette parties in the streets, where the bride would walk with her female friends and relatives and they would dress her up in costume and write remarks on her back making fun of marriage, its advantages and disadvantages, such as "Just Married," "In Training," "Girls Just Wanna Have Fun," and "Final Fling before the Ring." Temple Bar sometimes seemed quiet and sleepy, and at other times it was crowded and chaotic. In the middle there was a paved square with terraces like a Greek amphitheater, and the tourists, especially the Italians, would sit there singing and playing. They always joked with me and bought flowers from me. They also gave me food and drink. They would pass by every evening and we became rather friendly. A teenage girl from this group gave me a ring to remember her by and kissed me and said, "You'll be great one day." And I also gave her a ring to remember me by.

In the Temple Bar pubs, the locals drank till they were drunk. Then they would start singing. It was the popular songs that captured their emotions. They would sing "Whiskey in the Jar," or "I remember Dublin city in the rare ould times," or "You are my sunshine, my only sunshine, you make me happy when skies are gray."

They sang with gusto, especially the older people. With tears in their eyes, they crooned to the sound of the fiddle and coughed at the fug of cigarette smoke. It was as if something reminded them that the oppression of the past still had them in its thrall, as if the memory of English occupation still humiliated them and would inevitably defeat them.

They were enthusiastic about everything that was Irish and Celtic and very proud of their heroes and their martyrs, as if forgetting them would spell their demise and ruination. Music, poetry, and stories were the only way to survive, bearing historical witness to their existence.

At the end of the night the people of Dublin lined up outside Trinity College waiting for their turn to get into a cab, because they weren't allowed to drive when drunk. They looked like they were waiting for their turn in hell.

In summer the weather improved somewhat but the sky didn't stop howling and crying. The sun shone for about an hour or two every three days, then disappeared. I liked to walk in the streets downtown or go to St. Stephen's Green, a large park with a small lake on the banks of which live certain types of geese and ducks that I could not name. I wandered around there aimlessly. I looked at the flowers and the crows in the trees and remembered Ted Hughes, the English poet on whom I wrote my master's dissertation. He thought that humans were not very different from predatory animals in their aggressiveness and their unstable nature, and that in fact humans were sometimes more brutal than animals. He thought that animals killed to survive, whereas humans killed just to kill. What crime had the innocents who died in Nagasaki and Hiroshima committed? What crime have the hundreds who die in Palestine committed, or anywhere else where humans mistreat their fellow humans? Countries are fighting every day. Russia and Chechnya, Bosnia and Herzegovina, Kurds and Turks, Hamas and Fatah and the Martyrs Brigades, Kuwait and Iraq, England and Ireland, America and China and North Korea. Tyrannical governments, armies on the rampage, children killed with bullets through their skulls, bullets in the chambers of their hearts and the lobes of their lungs. Women raped. Wives widowed. Old men killed on pavements and in alleyways. The winner is humanity, and the loser is also humanity. A struggle to live and survive. Bloodshed. The angels have withdrawn their protective wings from Earth, and their predictions about the fate of mankind have come true. There are many questions and much speculation about the idea of man as God's viceroy on Earth.

I sat alone on the grass. I saw a young man and a young woman making love. The sight aroused me and I dreamed about it that night.

Britney still said nothing and kept on making the horse statues she liked to make. Mark had started to buy her cards for various occasions and put them on the kitchen table for her. The specter of Edna continued to haunt me for many days, especially after I saw her naked. She was like Eve walking in Paradise alone, looking for Adam. Patrick was in her room and I think she had just had sex and was on her way to the bathroom. I saw her and it was the first time I had seen a woman completely naked. Perhaps when I was a child I saw my mother's body as she bathed me. Despite all her years, Edna's body was the body of a woman of no more than twenty, in that everything was fresh and soft. She was half-drunk. She didn't see me of course. I saw her from behind.

I couldn't sleep and my head spun with thoughts: should I follow her into the bathroom? Had she also seen me naked before, when she walked in on me in the bathroom one night?

I had had a wet dream and I wanted to have a shower. In her eyes I read the surprise of discovering me. She didn't apologize but she looked at me, and perhaps she was horrified by the state I was in, or perhaps she was surprised that this childish face was attached to the body of a mature man, given how much hair he had on his chest, arms, and legs, and given what a strapping, well-proportioned body he had, and how strong he was despite his short stature. She may have discovered that the clothes that shielded me from the cold concealed wild lust and an amazing physique.

Joanna said, "Seamus Heaney is going to read some of his poetry in Dun Laoghaire next week." As she spoke her face was filled with delight, and the smile removed the wrinkles and sorrows of the years.

Her gray hair was streaked with black. Although the particulars of her body looked weak, overall she seemed extremely active. Her voice was weak but she was clearly audible. Her eyes welcomed me when I went into the office; she would meet me at any time and answer my questions even if she was busy, and she would remind the head of department what I was up to and what she had to do for me.

She described to me how to get to Dun Laoghaire, what number bus to take, where to catch it and where to get off. She finished it off by saying she hoped I would enjoy the party.

Despite the condensation on the bus window I was happy to be making this trip to Dun Laoghaire. I began to wipe the condensation off with my hand to see the beautiful, deep green that stretched as far as the eye could see and the neat houses that nestled lovingly in the fields. When I got off the bus there was a violent downpour, and I regretted that I hadn't brought my umbrella.

Seamus Heaney at last. For three years I'd been dreaming of meeting him and talking to him: an Irish poet who had won the Nobel Prize. Would I have a chance to meet him? The previous time I had visited Ireland I hadn't been able to meet him. I hadn't managed to travel to Cork, and the time had passed, and I was sad that I hadn't seen him. I had come to Ireland to find out what the Irish were like and write about their culture and history in a doctoral dissertation. James Joyce and Heaney were the examples I had taken as the starting point for my thesis.

I went into the hall. He was standing at the podium set up for him to read his poetry. Lights flooded the place in honor of poetry and the poet. He began to read "The Toome Road": "One morning early . . . ."

The reading ended, and the audience mingled in the reception hall. I was lost among them, not knowing what to do or how to talk to him. The silver trays came round with glasses of dark red wine, the color of blood that runs in healthy bodies. It was noisy and my voice quivered slightly, but I went up to him and introduced myself. I explained the subject of my thesis to him. Maybe he was pleased with what I told him; maybe he wasn't interested. Maybe he would have been more interested in me if I had met him ten years earlier, when no one had heard about him other than the Irish and some American academics, such as Helen Vendler at Harvard University.

I didn't have a camera to take pictures with him as proof that I had seen him and to document my trip to see him, but he said, "Next time you need to have a camera. We'll meet soon, don't worry, my Egyptian friend."

Chapter 26

The Northside of Dublin was completely different from the Southside. I think that's why the bridge was called the Ha'penny Bridge, because pedestrians had to pay half a penny to cross to the Southside where the rich people live. In front of the bridge there were bronze statues of two poor women: the Hags with the Bags. Northside Dublin was a deprived area. You would always see poor faces, drug addicts, and beggars, especially in O'Connell Street down which I strolled when I went to the General Post Office, when I visited my Algerian friend, or went to buy books from Eason's. Despite the poverty, there were some fancy shops and branches of famous brands. The Abbey Theater, founded by William Butler Yeats, Lady Gregory, and John Millington Synge as a national theater to contest English domination and to sound the trumpet call for a revival of the people's national consciousness, was also on the Northside.

The Moore Street Market, where I went to buy flowers if I couldn't find Frida and Rebecca at their usual place on O'Connell Bridge, was on the Northside. The street had plenty of flower sellers and a square where many types of goods were sold, and it was always crowded, especially on Fridays and Saturdays.

I once asked Frida if she could find me a place to live in this area, since it was close to the university. The house where I lived was very far from the university, and I had to stay in the street all day long until it was time to sell the flowers. I also felt that I was suffocating living with Edna. It was just that I felt lonely and bored in that house. She banned me from cooking at night and I'd had several arguments with her over food that she'd left and that I'd finished off at night out of extreme hunger. At first I didn't explain to Edna that I was selling flowers, to keep it a secret, but I later spoke to her openly about it.

I liked to walk in the college cloisters and to stroll on the extensive lawns, looking at the ancient buildings, especially the church. Once, when I wandered into the church, a man saw me and smiled. "Have you come to make confession or to look?" he asked. "I've come to find out," I replied. He began to talk about the origins of the church, about the fundamentals of Christianity and Christ's importance as the cosmic reformer, about the history of Catholicism in Ireland and its struggle with the Protestants and the English. Seven centuries of freedoms suppressed. Seven centuries of spiritual torment, seven centuries of penance for the blood of Christ. These people don't smile; they are sad for Christ, always atoning for Adam's original sin.

Christ's blood, shed on the cross, is still dripping and it hasn't yet wiped out their sins. That's why they drink so much and sing so much in Ireland.

I wasn't very focused on what he was saying. I was too busy calculating the angles of the light and how it came through the stained glass, and I began to count the wooden pews on the two sides of the nave.

I liked his white collar and his black cassock, a symbol of sadness, mourning, and self-denial. I remembered the vestments of the Coptic priests in St. Mark's Church in Old Cairo. I imagined myself wearing the cassock. I remembered that my friends at the Tawfikia School thought I was Christian because I looked like the priests.

I shook him off and went up to the department but didn't find Joanna. There was a short Scottish secretary who had a pretty face but whose mood was unpredictable. I missed Joanna. The secretary met me with a smile that was slightly scornful. That's how I read her

121

state of mind. I don't know. I'm always aware of people, and I sense at first sight whether they like me or hate me. Perhaps I'm wrong. I don't know. Perhaps that was her way of dealing with people in general. Not all those who smile at everyone are friendly.

I asked after Joanna.

"She's taken a year off," she said.

"Is she ill?" I asked.

"I don't know. You can get in touch with her."

Could I love a woman like Joanna? She was over fifty and I was less than thirty. Don't read kindness and duty as affection and love. Moataz, she's your mother's age. The nice security guard at the university told me as he drank his coffee that she was going to leave the department, because her health was frail. Her heart had let her down. The doctor had advised her to take a one-year break to recover her strength, and possibly to have an operation.

Joanna was the reason I was in Ireland this time.

I had met her when I first came to Ireland, on a short visit for a conference on Irish literature. Her face was cheerful and I told her I was from Cairo and had come to Ireland to attend a conference and collect some research material. She gave me the telephone numbers and addresses of literature professors who might be able to help me with the research I was doing.

I had gotten in touch with them and they had invited me to come to Ireland. She made sure that the letters I wrote to the department head reached her. If the other secretary had closed the door of their room and Joanna saw me from behind the glass, she would smile, rush to the door, bring me my mail and ask me how I was. She assured me that the weather would definitely improve.

She was always advising me to go to Belfast in Northern Ireland, which had had a different experience from Dublin because the political and religious conflict between Ireland, England, and the occupied north had its roots there. The Irish Republican Army was there—an organization that wanted to liberate Northern Ireland and unite it with the south after the two parts were divided because of the Anglo-Irish treaty that freedom fighter Michael Collins negotiated in 1921, and for which he paid with his life because the

IRA rejected the agreement. Twenty-six counties became the Irish Free State, while six northern counties remained part of the United Kingdom. Seamus Heaney was from County Derry in Northern Ireland. She joked and said, "There are plenty of the potatoes you like there too."

I got in touch with Joanna and she insisted on saying goodbye to me. I liked that.

We met at the back entrance to Eason's bookshop. It was summer and the sunlight was reflected in the rain puddles that still stood on the sides of the pavement. I found her standing next to the stairway leading to the bookshop. She looked pale, her short gray hair hanging limply over her faded cheeks, but her smile was radiant, defying life and the cruel weather. When she saw me, she stiffened nervously and put out her soft, warm hand.

"I've brought some students' papers on Seamus Heaney. They might be of use to you."

"Thank you very much. I'll miss you. I don't know what I'll do in this department when you're gone."

"You'll find someone else to help you."

"I doubt it, Joanna, you're perfect in every way."

"No, I'm human. If I was in Cairo and a foreigner, I'm sure I'd find someone to look after me. There are plenty of kind people in the world."

"How's your mother?"

"She's well. She's still eating the honey you gave her. You're generous, Moataz. No one but me is interested in her. She's over eighty but she understands everything. She feels for me and worries about my heart."

"No, you'll live a long time, Joanna. Heart ailments are a piece of cake these days."

She gave a bitter smile, then patted my hands.

We had tea in a cafeteria in one of the vast shopping malls. I was amazed by the bright yellow teapot; it was almost the color of sunflowers.

When she was next to me I felt that she was my lover and I wanted to share all my secrets with her, but I was tongue-tied and I ran out of things to say. Or that's how it seemed to me. She instinctively knew that this would be our last meeting.

I promised her I would see her regularly, but I didn't.

Chapter 27

Edna comes home drunk at night, unsteady on her legs, swaying right and left. She laughs hysterically. Patrick is a little more coherent, but his face has turned the color of a barrel of vintage wine. I hear the sound of the key in the lock, and I rush down the fifteen stairs to open the door for them, to save them their fumbling attempts to open it. She looks at me with weak eyes and stares. She says, "You're still awake. Did you make much money from the flowers today? You'll disappoint your mother. Did you come to get an education or to beg?" Then she laughs again. She goes into the kitchen, opens the fridge, then closes it, and pats my arm. The touch makes me think she's being affectionate.

"Patrick, aren't you going up to bed?"

"Not now," he replies.

She looks at me in surprise. I go up to my room and close the door. I look in the mirror and feel afraid. I cover the surface of the mirror with some pieces of underwear and sit down trying to write, fighting against fatigue and drowsiness. I write and write, then I get up and throw myself on the bed, feel an insect sting, take off the cover, and look for it. I hold it between my fingers. I don't kill it. I put it in a paper handkerchief and throw it in the trash.

I hear Edna's laughs coming from the room next door, coming through the wall.

I hear her moans. Her screams get louder, and her moans. After a while I'm restless, I feel uncomfortable. I go out. I go to the bathroom to have a shower to cool off, and my desire subsides a little.

Moataz, when you felt bored in Dublin, you would travel to lonely shores where there were no humans, such as the Galway coast, where no ships passed to break the desolation of the sea. You looked for a shop where you could buy an umbrella to protect your head and your body from the rain, which cleansed you so thoroughly that you have completely dissolved. You were also afraid of death by drowning. The children of Maria, the woman immortalized by Synge in his play *Riders to the Sea*, died here: absolutely none of them came back. They went to look for the unknown and discover its secrets. Were they able to bring back certainty? No, they all died. You were frightened of dying alone in this country.

On the seawall, made of cruel concrete, sat an old woman with her leg swollen from the cold and from disease, looking timidly at everyone who passed. In another spot, there was a man of over seventy walking languidly behind his dog, and throwing it some scraps from time to time.

The hot kisses that the lovers snatched on the beach put a stop to Moataz's tears and made him feel warm and less alone. The woman was jumping on the man's back and wrapping her powerful legs around him. He looked back and laughed and his face went red. He took the offensive, throwing her down on the sand and then jumping on top of her. She resisted and pushed him up. He ran after her and wrapped his arms around her, kissing her hungrily. She moved away and laughed, then they clung to each other firmly but tenderly, and with a deep kiss they brought to an end the scene that this stranger had directed in his loneliness, the stranger that was me.

"Do you know what I always used to dream of?" I said to Simone.
"What?"
"Of inspiring people to be good and to love, to renounce violence and live in brotherhood and peace. Of never seeing a child in tears, or an expression of contempt, or a drop of bloodshed without

126

justification. Of helping people on their way to the perfection that I lack. Of dying among people, peacefully, listening to words of love in the form of poetry or hymns. Of seeing angels smile at two moments, the moment of my end and the beginning of my last journey, and in the end I want the Earth to be the mother that encloses me."

"What's wrong with reaching this stage?" Simone asked me.

"For me," I said, "sin is sometimes a way to escape. It's the moment of truth when I admit that I'm human, that I'm weak, and that I'm asking for forgiveness and for life."

"This moment is what you have inherited from your religious ancestors," she said mockingly. "They were afraid of madness so they took refuge in unseen forces that made it easy for them to keep on living."

Defensively, I said, "No, there's an instinctive longing for fulfillment and immortality, to remain pure and clean."

Amazed, she put her hands firmly on my shoulders. "Romanticism has had a strong effect on you," she said.

"That's my problem. I'm always misunderstood," I said.

"Do you want to be rich?" she asked.

"I want to be happy," I said.

That caught her interest, and she said, "What's happiness?"

"Being content," I said.

"What's contentment?"

"Being satisfied with what God has given you."

"What I don't understand is why God created humans," she said.

"Have you read Milton's *Paradise Lost*?" I asked.

"You're paradise lost," she said, "but very often I don't understand you. You seem to have a puzzling personality, but I love you anyway. Sometimes I feel you're religious and as gentle as a child of less than three. But at other times, I feel there's a genie inside you that's fallen from the sky and wants to sow discord between people, that rebels against everything, that's so lecherous that it's vulgar, but so moral that it's puritanical and saintly. Sometimes you want to have the world and live life without limits, and sometimes you're so conservative you're ascetic, but then I love you anyway."

*

127

I grew fed up with living in Edna's house. The loneliness oppressed me. We didn't talk as much as we used to. She became more hysterical and neurotic. We argued for the most trivial of reasons: if I neglected her flowers, or if I ate some of her fruit, and she began to get annoyed with Patrick's conversations with me. "You'll annoy him by this talk of yours about Islam and what's allowed and what's forbidden, and about your beliefs, which I hate," she said. I decided to leave the house, although it was large and empty most of the time because Mark only came at night. We would exchange a few banal sentences such as "Simone called today, she's in love with you, beware of Irish women. Don't let them feel secure, because they're faithful, but as changeable as the Irish weather."

Yes, I often see Simone, but I have felt that she doesn't suit me, although she's kind-hearted. She thwarts every attempt I make to contact other women. Yes, I surrender my body to Simone, but my soul and my imagination are with Siham. I'm addicted to the sex dolls that adolescents and people deprived of women use to vent their repressed instincts and release their sexual tensions. As for my spirit, it's with her wherever I am.

I mentioned to Mark my idea of leaving the house. He welcomed the idea and said, "You'd do better to live near the university. That would save you time and effort."

I wondered why he didn't ask me to stay. Why did he insist that I look for somewhere else? Does he really want to get rid of me? Is he upset by my presence? Edna also welcomes me leaving! And it was she who suggested I leave the house in two months because there were some guests who were going to stay in my room. I knew that her friend with whom she escaped the orphanage in the old days was coming to live with her. So living together and friendship now counted for nothing. The opportunity had arisen for Mark to show his attitude toward me and for me to go far away, leaving the place to him so that he could live in peace in this house, which was calm before I came. He wouldn't be troubled by the idea of dying alone, as he had claimed.

I hadn't been annoying anyone, as far as I could tell. The routine of my life hadn't changed since I arrived: I wake up in mid-morning, perhaps at noon, make breakfast or put some clothes in the washing machine, read in the kitchen or translate some poems, watch the drum of the washing machine as it turned, go out into the back garden to look at the sky and the clouds that were building up, watch the little children that the woman next door looks after, say hello to them, bring in the washing when it looked like rain, then wash some of the dishes and dry my hands. Then I pick up my bag and put on my coat, walk a few yards, drop in on the post office to post some letters, catch the bus that comes every fifteen minutes, get on and smile at the driver, and look at the houses and their variously colored doors, the tall trees and all the delightful greenery.

I suddenly remember Hanan, then get off and walk pass the Bank of Ireland, then cross the street to the entrance to the university. I meet Mario, and we complain about the poor weather and dream of the sun of Rome or Alexandria. "We're relatives," I tell him. "Cleopatra and Antony were inseparable."

Mario is always smiling, and he always greets me with a 'salam aleekum'. When I hear it, it stops me feeling homesick. At this university, everyone is busy with themselves and their research. No one talks to anyone. The staff understand their jobs thoroughly, and all the students live in their own worlds. They study all day long, then go to the club or the bar attached to the university, or they go to bed. I walk alone in the dark square on campus, imagining the echo of the horses' hoofs, or the carriages ridden by English soldiers, or by the professors and students in the eighteenth and nineteenth centuries, before the independence of southern Ireland. I walk as far as the main gate with the wooden door. When I emerge from the narrow passage, I feel that I've come out of an impregnable fortress and that I have moved from one age to another. At the top of the building there's a large clock that always shows ten o'clock in the evening, the time I come out. I meet Mario and he says, "I'm going to meet a new girlfriend." He liked women and was always with pretty ones.

In the evening, I go back home, exhausted, with the cold crushing my bones, fearful of the specters that lurked in the tall trees, and the loneliness grows like mountains getting higher day by day.

In a hurry I wrestle with the key in the door, frightened of the echo of footsteps behind me, and breath a sigh of relief when I shut it. I take my coat off quietly so as not to disturb anyone. I make dinner from some scraps of bread and milk, and go upstairs. The dog barks when I accidentally step on its tail. It reminds me of the smell of infirmity, old age, and the gate to the tomb.

I go into my room and close the door behind me. I lie down on the bed, my limbs rigid. I wrap them in blankets, then read Ovid's *Ars Amatoria*. I dream of houris and of my beloved, who kissed every pore of my body. The houris hover around the ceiling and I'm amazed by the love-making positions that Ovid describes in his book. I feel that the origin of life is a love affair, physical intimacy between a man and a woman. I go to sleep embracing Ovid.

I met him by chance. He was standing next to the telephone kiosk with his gypsy hair hanging loose and free. He looked eastern. "Algerian?" I asked.

"No, Moroccan," he said. "I'm Adnan, and you?"

"Egyptian."

"What are you doing here?" I explained to him in brief, then told him I was looking for somewhere to live close to the city center. "I have a ground-floor apartment on the Northside," he said.

The Northside! Simone had warned me about that area, which had many poor and deprived people, as well as beggars and thieves. The Southside was more developed and more comfortable, but there was no chance of finding somewhere to live there. I didn't care. What could they do to me?

He gave me the telephone number of the landlord, then went off, warning me to tell the landlord that it was he who gave me the number. I didn't try to find out what that was about.

On the other side of the street I see Abu Alam, who is trying to speak to someone but can't make himself understood because he's speaking French, which he learned through a long history of oppression and occupation. The Irish speak English, and although they have gone through the same experience as the Algerians—attempts to kill off their language and bury their history—they can speak with all nations, so they haven't lost much because they have gained the language of the world. Moataz looks at the shops and the bars. He comes to a charity shop that raises money for people with Parkinson's disease. He goes into the shop. The saleswoman greets him with a smile. He wanders among the secondhand clothes on sale. He likes one of the coats. He looks in his pocket, though he knows very well what's in it—just twenty pounds. He reads the price on the coat sleeve—thirty pounds. These sick people deserved charity. They've lost their grip on things. Gravity plays tricks on them and their nerves are out of control. They've lost their hold on material things. Memories are the only things they can hang on to and that they don't forget. He hesitated to bargain with the saleswoman over the price of the coat. She might refuse. She might argue that she didn't have authority to reduce the price. She seemed like a kind woman with charitable inclinations; with her maternal instinct she realized that he only had twenty pounds.

She seemed to assess the whole situation and read his history from his eyes, his skin color, and how thin he was. She agreed. He handed her the money. He put on the coat, happy with his new garment, which would protect him from the biting cold of winter and stop his pains from spilling out onto the alien, soaked roadways. Perhaps a woman might take a liking to him and invite him to coffee in Bewley's, or a Guinness in the Bloody Horse after it's been renovated.

Chapter 28

The mirror in front of my desk frightened me because it showed me how I had changed since coming to Dublin. My face had been somewhat plump. The mirror showed me how much weight I had lost from not having enough food, from the energy I expended every day, from thinking about my family and how they were, and from the tension I regularly faced in the street. I would go to university from noon until sunset, then sell flowers from early evening until the middle of the night. When I came back I would cook some food, which usually burned because I was too busy with reading, which kept me busy till dawn. I often deliberately covered the mirror with a garment or a white sheet. Sometimes I would study my face in the mirror, in the hope of seeing the self I had lost because of this exile. I wanted someone to share this loneliness with me, even if it was only my shadow or my reflection in the mirror, which had started to swallow up my features day by day as details of my face and body drowned in it as in a deep sea. Although what the mirror reflected was accurate, I didn't believe it. I accused it of lying and of deception and I stuck my tongue out at it in scorn, and maybe in madness.

My hair grew longer. When I went past the barbershop in Nelson Street, I wanted to have my hair cut and reduce the weight on my head a little. But I always put it off for fear the barber would cut my throat with his razor or cut off my head while trimming my hair. I couldn't bear having a sharp instrument close to my skin or my scalp. Why not let my hair grow? It might give me strength like Samson. My willpower had grown weak, and my body had grown heavy from all the ideas, the delusions, and fears that had overrun it and piled up inside it.

One night I was frightened I might forget the face and body I had come here with, so I took Edna's camera, bought a Kodak film, went into my room, took off all my clothes, and took numerous pictures of many parts of my body. Then I stood in front of the mirror and took a photograph of my reflection in the mirror, completely naked.

I was thin and I was amazed by the thick hair around my private parts. "This is a violation of Islamic law," I said, because for three months no razor blade had come anywhere near this part of me. Apparently I had completely forgotten about my genitals and the instructions modeled on the practice of the Prophet Muhammad.

When I had the photos printed they were dark and my features were not clear in them, but I decided to keep them. I might lose myself completely. These pictures would help me recognize myself later, like an ancient Egyptian who had his body embalmed so that his spirit could come back to it one day and not mistake it.

A riddle:

Rebellious, with a devilish bent, a womanizer, untainted by impurities, with a clear conscience, chaste as an unborn child, an angel with wings, a demon with cleft feet, soft as the skin of women, hairy as an ape, fiery as hell, cold as ice, devout as a prophet, as freethinking as a libertine or an atheist, as sly as a fox, as predacious as a lion, as placid as a tortoise, as dull-witted as a fish, an articulate animal, a clown in the circus. Who am I?

As I went down the stairs carrying my bags, I encountered her. She looked exhausted or sick. She went into the living room and lay down on the sofa. She looked old. She had her eyes shut and her hand on her stomach, as if in pain. Her dyed hair was wet and stuck to her forehead. She avoided looking toward me, as if the life we had shared did not exist. I said, "Goodbye, keep well." She didn't answer, and I left the room in despair.

When Britney caught sight of me packing my bags and starting to move to the new house in the Northside, which was close to the university, she smiled. She came up to me and said, "I'm sorry if I caused you any trouble with my mother." She reminded me of the rice incident and said, "I don't want you to leave. You've created a wonderful life in this quiet house. By the way, my mother isn't happy with you leaving. She's depressed and in a bad mood." Then she said, "I heard from Mark that you like the statues I make. I wanted to ask you: are they really beautiful? I had serious doubts about what I was doing until I found out that you liked them." Then she said, "I was moved by having you with us and I made a statue for you. I'm sorry I didn't ask you for permission. Anyway, it's only a statue of your head. Did you know you look like the pharaohs, especially your face, your eyes, and your chin? I'll go up and fetch it and show you."

A statue of me? Why, I wondered. She came back looking cheerful and held out the bust to me. It looked just like me. It was like a bust of Napoleon Bonaparte or a Roman soldier. "Would you let me keep it to remember you by forever?" she said. "With great pleasure," I said. "Can I take a picture with you?" she asked. I welcomed the idea. I felt that she was lonely and neglected, an orphan though her father was alive and although her mother did take care of her. But what did she feel when her elderly mother was sleeping close to her room with another man, a man from the countryside, and coming out into the hallway drunk and naked on rainy nights? Britney would leave this house, for sure, and leave Dublin for another town in Europe, for Germany, her constant dream.

Chapter 29

I see him on my way to university. As massive and as strong as Hercules, with a golden complexion and hair. He leaves the buttons of his shirt open to show off his bulging muscles and the stiff hairs on his chest. He moves around with self-confidence, like the mayor of Dublin. He inspects the lanes of the city and asks after the inhabitants. At first I was frightened of him. I grew more frightened when I felt a desire to find out who he was. Once he bought some flowers from me and gave them to an Irish woman. He didn't kiss her immediately, which surprised me.

By repeated coincidence I would find him in O'Connell Street or near Bewley's coffee shop, wearing jeans that accentuated the musculature of his powerful legs. He wasn't smiling, but he looked at me and I paid no attention.

Once I met him in Parnell Square at the end of O'Connell Street. He was crossing the road and a speeding car almost hit him.

"Fucking Irish," he said.

So he wasn't Irish, I said. Perhaps he was drunk. There's nothing in Ireland but drink.

I went up to him and asked quizzically, "Where are you from?"

"I'm from Romania."

So another refugee.

"I thought you were Albanian."

He began to play with the hairs on his chest with his fingers.

"What are you doing in Ireland?" I asked.

"Everything."

My curiosity was aroused. Everything? How?

Many ideas occurred to me: a model for pornographic magazines, for example, a thief, a drug dealer.

Then he laughed and said, "There's no work for me here. In Bucharest everything was fine before the revolution. I worked as a pimp." I didn't show any surprise on my face. I think I had become emotionally numbed, but at the same time I respected his candor and his self-confidence. Personally, I can't speak openly about many things, especially to strangers.

"You've asked me a lot of questions, and I don't even know you," he said with a smile.

Then he said, "It doesn't matter. We'll get to know each other." "I often see you in Temple Bar selling flowers," he continued, "I like the way you sell and the way you talk. I think you make a lot of money. Know what? I wish I could do what you do, but nobody feels sorry for the likes of me, and the way I look causes problems."

Then suddenly he said, "What do you want from me? Do you like me? Don't worry. I'm easygoing and open to anything."

I was speechless. What could I say?

I wanted to run off far away, as I always did with men like him, but I found myself riveted. "Is he really so loose, so outrageous?" I said to myself.

I was frightened by his boldness, but I found myself confessing to him in the manner of a young child who has lost his way or is lost for words.

"I'm looking for someone to share my new place to live, because I'm going to rent an apartment, but the rent is extortionate and I want him to contribute to the rent," I said. "At university I found an advertisement from someone who wants to share, so I've come to speak to him. He lives near here, but I can't find the place."

"Where do you live?" he asked. "In the Northside, in Nelson Street," I said. "So we're neighbors," he said. Then he started to

136

describe the way to his house. Then he said, "Forget this person and this address. Come with me. I'll show you someone who'll share with you."

"Will you vouch for him?"

"Yes, take my word for it. He's from my city and he's dependable."

I was hesitant, but I agreed because I had to save some money and the rent was high. I would have no problem sharing the place with someone, but there was only one bed, big enough for a married couple maybe, but could I sleep next to a strange man who wasn't my brother or a relative? That would be hard.

Simone offered to share the place with me but I refused. I didn't want anyone to live at such close quarters with me in my loneliness.

He patted me on the shoulder and said, "Why are you thinking about it? Why the hesitation?"

We went to the end of Moore Street, where some Romanians were gathered speaking their language, which I don't understand. They all laughed when they saw me. He pointed at one of them and announced proudly: "This is your new roommate."

He was a young man in his thirties, slightly fat with a touch of jaundice in his crossed eyes. "What do you think?" he said.

I was embarrassed and I hesitated to reply.

"Give me your address and I'll come by tomorrow to tell you what I decide," I said.

I knew I was lying but it was just an attempt to escape.

After his friends left us, I stayed with Hercules and I felt that he didn't want to part from me, as if he abhorred a vacuum and he wanted to overcome it by having me for company, so he invited me to have a coffee, since the weather was cold and rainy.

We went together to his apartment. I was gripped by fear. He did all kinds of work. He might be a thief or a murderer. He might kill me. He might try to rape me. "Don't be frightened," I said to myself, "What will he do to you? You're a man like him, and he's a pimp, so he won't do you any harm." When we were inside his house, he took off his shirt, and the muscles in his chest, his back, and his shoulders were clearly visible.

"Your apartment's not bad," I said.

"It's expensive," he said. "Three people from the village I come from live here. I'm looking for private houses for them. The Irish government will pay their rent and other costs only when they find a place and an address."

"You seem to be working as mayor for all the Romanians here," I said with a laugh.

"Living in Romania is very hard these days," he said. "The fall of communism after Ceauşescu was executed was a disaster. Bucharest was devastated, full of corruption, so I left. Also, I can't work in Ireland. The Irish Garda are on the alert."

He made me a coffee.

As he handed it to me, he said, "I sleep on this couch. One of the others sleeps on that sofa, one sleeps on the floor, and the third in the kitchen."

The sound of trucks driving past the house, shaking it. The sun had gone down and night had fallen. Some drops of water spattered on the windowpane, heralding rain. I stood up. He faced me too. We were face to face. He was taller than me. My body was dwarfed alongside his broad frame, and I could no longer see anything. I asked to leave. He went ahead of me with slow steps, and said, "I'll be waiting for you."

When I tell Frida, "Don't throw the rose stems into the river so you don't pollute it," she says, "Aren't we all polluters?"

Frida doesn't like the smell of the River Liffey. She says it smells rotten. Then Rebecca turns to me and says, "Moataz, I want you to write a letter to Dublin city council. I want them to leave me alone. They arrest me every day, and that bunch of cowardly men and women force me to pay a fine before they let me go." She spits, then a policeman turns up and she stops speaking. He speaks to Rebecca in rather a gentle way and with a smile he orders Frida and her to move along.

"An admirer," I tell her.

"Handsome, isn't he?" She laughs wickedly.

"Do you want to go out with him?"

"No, I love my husband. I have five children with him but I can't ignore looks of admiration and respect from polite men, because they don't treat me like the whores who work with him in the police force. I despise all of them because most of them come from the bog." Then she straightened up as she dictated the letter to me:

Dear official,

I grew up in the city of Dublin. Here by the River Liffey and in the streets of the city my mother, a flower seller who never taught me any other trade, cried her wares. I spent a few years in the city's schools, not learning anything, but in the streets I learned much. We are not a disgrace to the state, sir. By class we are the toiling poor, and we do a lot for this country. We sell the most beautiful things the earth produces, the most splendid symphony of colors from the flowers created by God. I implore you. I want to live peacefully with my children and my husband and earn an honest living. All the nationalities that have recently poured in on us after our years of isolation come to see us and take pictures of us. We are poor flower sellers, the honorable face of rainy Ireland. I am responsible for five children and my only helper is this cart filled with delicate spirits. It is drugs, not flowers, that you should be confiscating and banning. Why do the police chase us away? Why don't they give us permanent licenses to sell so that we can be spared such humiliations? I beseech you in the name of God and the Virgin Mary to listen to us and let us sell flowers in the street.

Yours sincerely, Rebecca

She dictated the letter to me, but I decided to keep it. I promised her I would write it out on a computer, print it, and put it in a smart-looking envelope. I read it to her time and time again, and she was delighted with the letter and the effect it had on me, especially when I told her that she had a fine literary style.

I took the letter from her and kept it, but I didn't print it. Maybe I forgot, maybe I felt there was no point in sending it, and she too only asked me about it once.

Then autumn came, promising a fierce and bitter winter. Strong, cold winds shook the flowers violently and they fell dead on their grassy graves.

I wore all the clothes I had and bought a raincoat and a new pair of Clarks shoes. I cut my hair short after buying a new pair of scissors. I bought a woolen hat, and by chance I came across a yellow Benetton scarf lying near someone's house. I prepared myself for winter's brutal arrival.

Simone imposed herself on me with full force, and I surrendered. I admitted point-blank that I didn't love her and I said I was just a man who has needs and wants consummation, a man who has met a woman who wants to compensate him for the deprivations and homesickness he has suffered and perhaps to find out more about this stranger. When she was drunk she told me that I wasn't the first Arab in her life, but she had been in love with some Moroccan who worked in Dun Laoghaire in a fish-and-chip shop on the sea. I think that if I left her she wouldn't lose much. She admits that her friend Brendan is a political activist who thinks that revolution is the answer and that he might involve her in acts of violence, while she thinks that singing world music will solve the problems of racism, occupation, and injustice in the world. She's always complaining about her English friend, who makes fun of her and rejects her control over and leadership of the singing group. I always interpret this conflict between them politically, because the story of England and the ethnic and sectarian conflict in the occupied north is a history of superiority and inferiority complexes. I felt that Simone was the underdog. She was struggling to make things work and not to contradict herself by advocating singing as a force for peace while simultaneously hating and being jealous of her English friend. But what if this English woman really was as Simone imagined and looked with contempt at everything that was Irish, particularly Simone?

"Could I have a chicken combo meal please?"

I handed the cashier a twenty-pound note. She looked at it carefully and marked it with a red pen, which made a faint line. She looked at me suspiciously and said, "I'm sorry, sir, I can't accept this note."

Naively, I asked her why not.

"Because it's a forgery," she said.

The night before I had realized it was a forgery from the way it felt, the poor quality of the printing, and the thinness of the paper. That was after rain fell on it and it got wet. I had three banknotes I'd been given by a young man who bought three flowers from me. Or perhaps I received them from Hercules the Romanian, I don't know, because he had also bought some flowers from me. The street was dark and I was delighted he had paid more than the usual price for a flower. I suspected it might be a forgery but I offered it to the cashier anyway. He had tricked me, so I had to trick them—not a principle I've used much in my life, but loneliness and hardship had taught me a lot.

The three policemen put me in a police car, and for the first time I saw the real cruelty of the police. I tried to explain who I was and what I was doing there. I took out my papers but they weren't interested. I hid my Trinity College identity card.

In the police station they put me in a room by myself and took all my money from me.

I decided to explain my situation to them honestly. I was terrified. The next day they would contact the head of the department at the university.

A beggar, a flower seller working on a doctorate. They wouldn't appreciate that I need the money. They'll say, "Why didn't you go back to your own country if you don't have enough money to live among us?" They wouldn't respect me if I told them that I refused to seek welfare from the Irish government as many other foreigners do. I refused to apply for recognition as a political refugee or as someone persecuted for their religious beliefs. I was full of pride in myself and in my roots.

In the room, which was lit by fluorescent lights, I recited the Yassin and the Joseph chapters of the Qur'an, and remembered how Joseph spent years in prison, unknown to anyone but his companions, whose future he predicted. Perhaps I will end up crucified, with birds eating from my head, my death witnessed by a group of people and crows, who may rejoice, or may grieve, at the fate that has befallen me. It would be hard, it would even give one sleepless nights, to know one's own fate, especially if it was death and annihilation. How did Joseph's companion get through the night after Joseph interpreted his dream for him? Perhaps he didn't believe it. Perhaps he said, "Wild fantasies," or perhaps he didn't take any notice at all of the interpretation, and he just fell asleep from exhaustion and fatigue, but how will I get to sleep? Perhaps I'll be imprisoned here forever. No one will know anything about me. I'll never see my mother again, or my sisters, or my beloved.

No one would see the money I had saved and put on top of the wardrobe in my room for fear of theft. No one would benefit from it, neither my relatives nor I. I would die in prison and they wouldn't know who I was. The money would be wasted or another tenant would take my room, including the books and the money in it.

Who but the Lord would free me from this prison?

"O Lord, set me free." I prayed as my father taught me to pray when I was in trouble. "You have imprisoned me. Now set me free from every trial and tribulation that afflicts me."

I began to bang on the cell door as hard as I could. It was a steel door. No one answered.

A few moments ago I was free as air. Now I was in chains. I remembered a saying by some philosopher: "How precious you are, O freedom."

There was a horrible smell that blocked my nose. It came from a toilet, and on the side there was a small bed with a dirty mattress. I tried to sit down but I was frightened of the mattress. I began to bang on the door with all my might and begged them to let me go, because I was the victim of a trick, and if anyone should be imprisoned it was the Irish criminals who had forged these notes.

I had visions of my life, from childhood till I found myself in jail. I had visions of the students I used to teach and the teachers who taught me in Cairo, of my family and friends, and how I ended up as a peddler wandering the streets and lanes, carrying flowers in my arms to sell to passers-by and the clientele of bars and pubs.

I was exhausted from banging and calling the police. Then they opened the door and said, "You can make a telephone call." I didn't

142

have anyone to call. Simone couldn't come and get me out of this situation. Frida and Rebecca didn't have telephones and I didn't know their addresses. I felt I was alone, imprisoned in the police station with my nightmares. Suddenly a young man appeared and the officer introduced him to me as a lawyer. Then the officer said, "Speak with him. It'll do you good."

I told him my story. He laughed and said, "Take it easy!" Then he left.

They released me after four hours and gave me notice to appear in court on Wednesday, August 5, to meet the judge, who would hear what I had to say about the charge against me: the charge of forgery.

I came out of solitary confinement, suddenly aware of the value of freedom. I was frightened, tense, and alone. I was frightened that at any moment the police might re-arrest me on the forgery charge. What would happen to me? Would they convict me? Would they sentence me? Would they deport me to Cairo for forging banknotes and begging? I began to walk uneasily down the Dublin streets. I wanted to stop people in O'Connell Street or Moore Street to tell them my story. I wanted to say to them, "Come with me and let me show you that I'm innocent and good and I couldn't have forged this money." I would tell them that I don't like money in the first place and that my aim was knowledge, not material things. There was a week to go before my court appearance. Why not go away? Why not go back to Cairo? Why stay here? But I hadn't finished my research. Also I wanted to clear myself of this baseless charge. I wouldn't go back to Cairo till I'd finished my thesis and saved enough money to buy a ticket back to Cairo. When I told Mario, he told me, "You could escape to Northern Ireland. It's another country." I said I would go to Belfast but I would definitely come back to Dublin, because I wasn't a coward.

"You hurried to climb to the top of the wardrobe to pick up the money hidden there. You need to keep it in a safe place so you decide to put it in a bank account until you have enough for a ticket home, and you give the account number to your brother in Cairo in case you're imprisoned or die."

143

Before I went to Belfast, Frida said to me, "You have to go to the Four Courts Buildings at the appointed time, or else the police will have to arrest you and put you in the mixed prison, whatever the mixed prison might be!" There would be drug addicts in there, some of them thieves. Maybe, if you were lucky, they would force you to get addicted too, or rape you if you were pretty and sexy, or kill you if worst came to worst.

I imagined myself in a closed room, surrounded by men everywhere, unable to defend myself. That would be the end, and I couldn't live one day longer, the day I lost my manliness.

Chapter 30

Belfast is drowning in rain. Dark, lonely streets, with no one moving, nothing astir. It lies silent under the umbrella of the Great British Empire. I imagined it as a different city, full of activity and revolution.

I arrived late. It was raining as usual. I stood in Ulster Street, trying to think of a reason for leaving Dublin and coming to Belfast. I had a strong and insistent desire to see a different city. Politics and struggle were here, and not in Dublin. I remembered my friends' warnings to avoid the city because it was a hotspot of violence, but nothing ventured, nothing gained. The city wasn't very different from Dublin. The sky was always oozing the rains that create life and make the ground shake and grow, but all I could see was green grass so dark that it was almost sad. Faces with no expression other than a certain restlessness as they tried to read my nationality without asking what color my passport was. Or perhaps they were provoking me by their silence, silently shouting out, "He's come to take our money, he's going to commit outrages," whereas I was very far from doing such things because I was obsessed with other things.

I was obsessed with things to be found maybe on Earth, maybe in the sky, maybe in the world of Platonic forms. Here I was walking through the shopping district, looking at the shops, the clothes, whether expensive or cheap. I had breakfast in a fast food restaurant. I walked past the parliament building. I came across a group of young men. I avoided looking at them, but nonetheless, they made derogatory remarks about me being a foreigner and an Arab. I answered them in silence. "You ingrates, you think the whole world is like you. You look at the color of people's skin. You ogle their bodies, sometimes with contempt. You care about appearances and ignore what's inside. You like tradition and you hate whatever is new. You sleep like sheep in the embrace of your women, who are hungry for love and bread, while you forget to look up at the sky. Maybe you are the ones who took part in the mass trial of all your distinguished countrymen and your men of literature. Anyone who was different from you, you stoned. There was Patrick Kavanagh, whose poetry you ignored and who died a depressed alcoholic after writing his famous poem *The Great Hunger*, which conveys the protagonist's psychological and physical deprivation and how he was so frightened of his mother that he masturbated in the fields for fear his mother might see him doing it at home.

"Maybe it was you who didn't ask Joyce to stay in Ireland instead of having to tramp around Zurich and Paris. You forced him to leave through your neglect. He wrote the history of Dublin, your city, as if he were Herodotus, creating a modern epic from your disappointments, your failures, your betrayals, your rejoicings, and your misery, from your food and drink, your covenants, your dances, your defeats, the joys of your women, the types of trousers you wear, your tensions, the impulses of your lust, the temperament and physical experiences of your women, the names of your streets, the type of clocks you have, the style of your architecture and of your furniture. *Ulysses*, your great narrative and your eternal epic, was not written among you, but far away in Trieste, somewhere warmer than Dublin. You didn't care whether he lived among you or not! Were you so busy with major issues and with great historical transformations that you ignored your men of literature, and abandoned them to loneliness and delusion? Didn't you ask where he was or how he was living, whether he was being creative or not? You weren't interested in him as a person and you paid no attention to his creativity. You didn't console Joyce when he was struggling with his daughter's madness and his own blindness. Despite that, he wrote his third novel, *Finnegan's Wake*, a kind of lament for the state of Ireland."

I came to my senses to the sound of rain falling on my face. It soaked me like a raging torrent. I imagined that it would swallow me up and I would die drowned in the land of rain. Where's the pleasure in coming to this city, I wondered. A long, endless road with only three or four men on it. I spotted a car parked by the station. A woman was sitting in it. As soon as I spoke to her she panicked. She didn't wind down the window. She just pointed with her hand. I realized that she didn't know the place I had asked her about. I was frustrated and I asked myself the eternal question: "What brought me here?"

I looked for a restaurant where I could have dinner, which would double as my lunch. I walked a considerable distance. I asked for restaurants and I found out that there was a Kentucky Fried Chicken not too far off.

"A chicken meal, please."

"Sauce, rice, Pepsi?"

"No."

"Anything else?"

"No, thank you."

"Seven pounds."

I handed her the money.

She looked at me indignantly. "We don't take Irish money," she said. "We only deal in sterling."

"Why?" I asked.

"This is Northern Ireland. We're part of the United Kingdom," she said.

"But it's still Ireland, isn't it? And you're Irish?"

"I'm English," she said.

She sent her friend to deal with me.

My attempt to persuade them to accept Irish money came to nothing.

I was forced to go and change some money, so I wandered the streets looking for a money changer or a bank that was open at night.

It was a frightening city. It went to bed early. Classical buildings. The Northern Ireland Parliament building in all its grandeur.

The mansions built by the English aristocrats in the eighteenth and nineteenth centuries, bearing testimony to the splendor and strength of the empire. I remembered Edward Said and his book *Culture and Imperialism*. I imagined the Khedive Ismail ordering foreign architects to build the city center in both the French and the English styles. I almost fell over when I was looking at the buildings and my feet slipped because of the rain. The rain seemed to be working against me and ruining my trip deliberately. It pelted down and I tried to hide from it in a telephone booth. The rain seemed to assail the road with cruelty and violence and the water began to clatter on the asphalt like the feet of a modern dance troupe on a large wooden stage—not a pretty sight because the dance was set to a rhythm that was random and feverish.

I went into a pub where there were a few men and women. One of the men noticed me when I went in and wouldn't leave me till I was his guest in a haunted house down a dark alley. He was the only person who offered to put me up when I failed to find a modest hotel where I could seek shelter from the cold and the heavy rain. Strangely, I didn't know why he had invited me to his house or why I agreed to go. Why am I so susceptible to strangers? And why am I so reckless in my quest for experiences? He might have been a criminal who wanted to rob me or kill me after failing to make me submit to him. I wonder if I have some other, secret motives for being so obliging toward people whose identity I don't know. I'm well aware that I refuse to get involved in any relationship that I don't feel completely comfortable with, but other people don't understand that, especially foreigners, because if you go into someone's house there's an implicit agreement on what will happen next, whatever that might be. Sometimes it's no good trying to communicate with other people or to share a special moment of existential unity with them.

The owner of the house went upstairs to sleep, tired out from drinking and sadness. I remained alone except for a weird cat that started to rub against me, seeking protection. Its eyes frightened me and I freaked out. I opened the door and rushed out into the unknown, afraid of myself and of the cat. I looked for a taxi to take me to the nearest hotel.

I came to a youth hostel and stayed in a room where I couldn't work out who was sleeping where because the light was so faint. There were many bunk beds. I couldn't get to sleep until daylight broke. A woman threw her underwear in my face unintentionally, and I saw something that my eyes had never seen before and that I had never imagined happening. I heard the sound of the water hitting the pores of her skin as she showered. When she came out she shared a deep kiss with her boyfriend, who was twice her height.

In the daylight the city was completely different. It seemed reborn. The car horns, the voices of the passers-by, the laughter of the children, the colors of the clothes, and the way they merged with people's bodies, the symmetrical buildings, the friendliness of the people. The bookshop owner spoke warmly about the East and Egyptian civilization: with pride he said his best-selling books were books on Pharaonic civilization. In the end he gave me several books as a gift, as a token of friendship between the Irish and the Egyptians. For some reason I remembered Hanan and said that when I went home I would give some of them to her.

Belfast is a fine city but how could I live there for any length of time? I'd like to stay there for a month as had already been decided and as I had told Joanna. But how? How could I save up the money? Because I had work in Dublin, and life was safer and more lively there.

I wandered though the corridors of Queen's University and saw statues of the writers who had studied there. I went into the library and browsed through some of the reference works. This is the university where Seamus Heaney studied; they are very proud of him. I wondered whether my university would one day appreciate me as the West does its poets and writers.

Tomorrow I have to go back to Dublin, because I have to go to court to meet the judge.

O beautiful Belfast, I have to leave you and go back to Dublin, where prison, humiliation, and disgrace await me.

Chapter 31

The Court

I started looking for the court. The weather was clear and, unusually, the sun was shining. Its light filled the air. The streets were empty in Dublin's Northside. I thought the court was on the banks of the Liffey, but they said it was close to Church Street, in Chancery Place to be precise. On both sides of the street there were buildings that looked like the low-cost housing the appliance company Ideal had built in the Cairo suburb of Shubra. When I arrived I asked the guard where the courtroom was. "There are many courtrooms," he said. "That's why it's called the Four Courts. Which courtroom do you want?" Then he asked me what I was charged with and I told him what had happened. The guard smiled and said, "Go up to the second floor."

There were indeed many courtrooms. I chose one and went inside. I was surprised to find large numbers of people coming out, and the judges leaving the bench. I was unsure what to do.

Then I went to the other courtroom and sat down. What was my crime? And where was my address to the judge? And where was the lawyer? What was the case number? Where was the prosecutor? And so on.

The room was full of people, most of whom looked like Northside people—refugees and foreigners. I noticed my Romanian friend.

I thought of going and sitting next to him and talking to him about the counterfeit banknotes. Perhaps he would testify on my behalf with a straight face. But I preferred not to let him see me in this situation.

Suddenly a woman in lawyer's robes turned up, apparently in the final month of pregnancy. The judge would ask the defendant if he had a lawyer, and if he didn't have one he would ask the defendant to choose one. Strangely most of them chose this woman.

The judge called the woman who was sitting next to the Romanian. She stood up and said, "Yes, Your Honor, I did steal. But it was against my will. The shampoo I stole was made in my country and it reminded me of my mother, who always used to buy me this shampoo in Romania. When I saw it I felt my hand reaching out and picking it up, and in it I could smell my mother as she washed my hair when I was a child. Now I stand before you confessing my mistake."

The woman lawyer then stood up and said, "Your Honor, she's a refugee, in exile and poor, and stealing shampoo is not a mortal sin. The fact that she missed her mother was stronger than her sense of right and wrong. Forgive her, for Jesus' sake, and she'll swear not to do anything like that ever again." She told the woman to stand up again and the woman swore as the lawyer had instructed her.

I was delighted she was acquitted. I hoped this same lawyer would defend me when my turn came. She would tell them that I didn't present the banknote to the cashier deliberately, that I wasn't responsible for counterfeiting this money in Ireland, and that I didn't even know where it came from; that I was a doctoral student performing significant services to Irish culture in the Middle East and that I was innocent. You are the forgers, go look for them among your own and put them on trial.

I was about to stand up and shout in the judge's face: "What crime have I committed? Why have I come here?"

But the judge interrupted me. Then a handsome man, who was of medium height and looked to be in his mid-thirties, stood up. "Why do you beat your wife?" the judge asked him. "What kind of man beats his wife? What if you were to kill her, when she's the mother of your child, when she looks after your home and fills it with light?"

"Milord, she's a liar," said the man. "I never beat her, but I tell her to stop shouting in my face and being suspicious of the way I behave toward other women. She's always arguing for the most trivial of reasons and is jealous even of my relatives and my nieces. Nothing makes her happy. She doesn't even like the gifts I give her. She says I have poor taste. And she's always complaining to her family that I'm stingy with money and food, although in fact all I do is try to please her. She argues about everything. She has a bizarre urge to drink large amounts of milk, and I understood that because she was nursing her baby. She only likes to argue late at night. Her mother treats me rudely, and her father deliberately threatens me. He thinks she's as meek as a Siamese cat, but she's quite the opposite.

"I love her and I often tell her I love her. On our wedding night, I told her, 'After the existence of God, the second truth is that I love you.' I can't bear her being away because sometimes she's kind and she knows how to make me forget my worries, and on top of all that, God has graced me through her with a child who has saved me from the madness of loneliness and isolation, but she exploits my good nature to get the better of me and to make sure her word prevails."

Then he added, "Your Honor, my wife claims that I treat her violently, but to tell the truth, I don't get in her way unless she provokes me. By nature I'm calm and thoughtful, because I'm a writer and I have written some novels that have been distributed on a limited basis, and I'll give you some of them."

"A colleague of mine," I said to myself, "I should get to know him if he's lucky enough to be acquitted."

He passed the judge some of his books. The judge looked at the novels and smiled.

"I like peace and quiet," the man said, "but she's always arguing for the silliest reason, and she never thanks me for anything.

"I've always written her poems, and I've always given her flowers. The last time we argued it was Valentine's Day and I had brought her some flowers, but she threw them aside and wasn't interested, and the flowers wilted. There's a witness, my son John."

152

"Where's John?" asked the judge.

"Your Honor," said the lawyer for the plaintiff, "this is the boy." John was an infant of a year and a half, and the courtroom laughed.

"She doesn't know I love her and I can't do without her," said the man. "She and my son are the lights of my life. They are the sun and the moon in the dark skies of my life. She wants me to love only her, and this is selfish. I love all mankind. No one in her family treats me fairly and everyone is against me and they only listen to her.

"Be fair to me, Your Honor, and have pity on my situation, because I want to live happily with my son and bring him up properly and help him with my money and my culture, please."

The judge looked at the man and said, "Acquitted." Then the judge stood up and left. The defendant hugged his wife and child and there was uproar in the courtroom. Then people left the room. I stayed alone, not knowing what to do. Would the court resume or not?

After a while I went outside and asked one of the staff. "How can you come to court without any papers or a policeman?" they said, "Go back to the police station and ask about the charge against you."

I went back to the police station and asked the policeman, who didn't seem to understand anything and looked tired, perhaps from drinking all night. I told him what had happened in court but he said, "Don't worry."

"Won't I have to go to court another time?" I asked. He didn't answer. Then he left the room, leaving me alone.

Then he came back and said, "You're lucky. Your charge documents went missing and didn't go to court. Off you go: you're free."

Of course I was free. I wasn't guilty of any forgery offense or of circulating counterfeit currency. That money came from you and was yours. You made it and circulated it, but you're clever enough to cover up your crimes and wise enough not to open closed doors and light fires. Money laundering and European Union deals and so on. Thank God the documents went missing, and I didn't get lost with them.

Chapter 32

Things are getting worse on the streets. The rain is pouring down, the cold is freezing everything, and the Russian coat is no good because it restricts one's movement. Violence reaches its peak. You've started to get upset for trivial reasons and to clash with racist customers and tramps as well. One of them took some money from you and promised to get you a gold trinket. You thought you'd keep it for your mother. But he didn't produce the trinket but ran off with it and you didn't tell the police because you knew him and you had been friends. As he sat next to the Bank of Ireland, you told him that you were a lad from Shubra and that he didn't know what it meant to be a man. But his wife promised that she would give you back the money. But she blamed you for what happened, saying, "How can you expect money from a morphine addict?" A woman slapped you on the cheek because you pressed her and the woman she was with to buy flowers. She thought you were hitting on her friend. A drunken vagrant injured you when he grabbed a flower and gave it to the woman he was with. You ran after him to get the flower back and he hit you with the pail you put the flowers in. You started to hang out next to the walls, hiding in the Merchant's Arch passageway, begging and weeping bitterly, wanting to go back to your country, and at night you hug your pillow and long for love and comfort.

You started to invite women and men to your house and then throw them out when they misunderstand you. You don't dare to act directly, but instead you make do with devious, roundabout practices such as voyeurism. The landlord almost threw you out one night when you had an argument with a woman guest who was drunk and who woke up the other residents because you wanted her to take off her clothes so that you could have the pleasure of looking at her body. She refused and screamed because you hadn't given her the money you had agreed to give her, even though you hadn't had sex.

You serve yourself the food you've cooked: some lamb, because you're afraid of beef and there's the scare over mad cow disease all over Europe, especially Ireland. You bought the lamb from Marks and Spencer's and said, "I'll cook a feast today." You hoped that someone would join you, as Christ used to do with his disciples. You sat down and remembered that you hadn't recited "In the Name of God" over the food, because it wasn't halal: in fact you're eating carrion. You hadn't bothered to go to the South Circular Road to buy halal food. You chewed it and then you felt sorry for yourself and you felt as if you were crying inside and the tears were mixing with your flesh. So you spat out what you had in your mouth and your eyes were bathed in tears. Then you went into a fit of weeping and sobbing and you almost lost consciousness because your heart is so weak. Then you looked up to heaven and prayed to God to forgive you. You asked yourself, "Are you a believer?" Then you said you were alone and weak. Then you said that divine providence was protecting you, and you said that you were stronger, fortified by God's Book, as your father used to say.

But was there any faith on my part? My faith was incomplete, because I neglected to pray, but my heart was full of love. Even when I sin, God is very close to me. My guilt connects me and elevates me to Him. But I hide myself in embarrassment and shame and, like the first Adam, I look for leaves in the garden of Eden with which to cover my private parts. In my loneliness, God is present, reassuring me. I even need to be alone in order to be with Him.

*

It's raining as usual and the temperature is falling. I imagine Dublin as an Ice Age city: the faces pale white from the cold, the old women walking down the street, struggling with the rheumatism that has increased with the cold weather. Next to the wall of the Bank of Ireland the beggars are fighting off the cold with blankets and more layers of clothing. They close their eyes from the cold. Maybe they're convinced that it spells death and the eternal afterlife. I looked at my fingers and the pharaonic blood had drained out of them. They had been frozen by the bitter Irish climate. I had finished reading and had left the Lecky Library. I hadn't expected it to grow dark so early and to get so cold, although Simone had warned me in the morning. She had advised me to leave the fire on all night, and to wrap myself up well, because the Irish cold was deadly, but my contempt for nature got the better of me.

Suddenly I felt hungry. I remembered that I hadn't had breakfast. I checked my pocket. I only had ten pounds in my pocket. I would have fish and chips from the fish and chip shop. It might help the blood flow through my veins.

I would have a glass of beer. I talked myself into that. On the way I noticed the kind woman I always saw standing next to the soup cart, which was just a van with a kitchen inside containing a pot with soup that they gave out on cold days to anyone passing by. The woman was always smiling at me and offering me a bowl. I tried to warm my hands with the heat of the soup, and the soup rushed hot inside me, and I felt warm. On one side of the van I read, "Remember the Great Famine 1845–52. God curse you, Trevelyan. You were in power and you misgoverned."

"Trevelyan was in charge of the treasury.
An Englishman in control of Irishmen.
What did he say? Having too much spoils the slaves
While austerity will teach them many lessons.
This is philosophy, not economics,
But what's the use of remorse?
Because of him millions of Irish died hungry.
Amazing."

The woman told me she often saw me selling flowers, and she wanted to speak to me, but she was too embarrassed and felt that I was busy. She said she was doing charity work, and I said, "That's very good of you." She said, "Would you like to join us and volunteer?" "With great pleasure," I said. "On Sunday we'll go to church together and I'll introduce you to my friends. Please give me your address and I'll come by." "What's your name?" I asked. "Rose," she said.

Chapter 33

O Lord, if my sins are great in number,
I have learned that your mercy is greater,
If only those who do good can appeal to You,
then to whom should sinners turn for help?
I appeal to you humbly, O Lord, as you have commanded,
and if you turn me away, then who will have mercy?
I have no way to reach you other than through hope,
the grace of your mercy and the fact that I am Muslim.
Abu Nuwas, *The Sinner's Prayer*

Rose came on time to take me to her church. I opened the door for her and took her to the new room I had rented in Nelson Street. The smell of her perfume filled the place. I noticed that she had bright polish on her fingernails. Her fingers were delicate and enticing.

"Bright colors make you more beautiful," I said.

I sat down and felt a strong desire to embrace her. "Be prepared," I said to myself. I made her a cup of coffee and played the Amr Diab song "Here's the innocent angel" on the cassette player. I explained to her what the words meant.

"Unlucky in love?" she said.

"Like all of the few romantics left in the world today," I said.

"Divine love will make you overlook those minor matters."

"And the body? And the ache of desire?"

"You can overcome them by transcending them and by giving."

"And sin?"

"Christ cleansed us of sin by bearing the cross."

The more she spoke about religion, the more I desired her. The devil seemed to be playing a malicious game, but only with me.

"We should go to church," she said. "We'll be late."

I moved closer to her. The bed was in front of us.

She caught sight of a Qur'an that was lying peacefully next to my pillow. "What's this book?" she asked. I told her it was the Qur'an. "Can I look through it?" she said. Is she ritually clean? Or is she menstruating? Only those who are ritually clean can touch this book. "Let me hold it while you look," I said, and she was surprised. "Why won't you let me look through it?" she asked. "I like the decoration on the cover," she added. I took the Qur'an in both hands and offered it to her. "I'd like to hear you reading from it," she said. "I love strange languages, especially Arabic." So I began to read the Yassin chapter to her.

I saw her listening with interest, even if she didn't understand the words. Then she said, "Translate for me what you're reading." I tried hard to translate the verses.

"We're no different from you," she said. "We're similar to the point of being identical. The essence is the same—to worship God and help human beings to be at peace with themselves and with others. We're against everything that's vulgar and sordid. We fully believe that God exists and that He calls on us to be righteous and pure so that people can reach the peak of humanity to which they aspire. We don't touch alcohol. We don't want fornication and adultery to be people's normal behavior. We're seeking the true nature of mankind in its original form. The state of perfection, with no imperfections. Those verses you read me are exactly what we believe and what we strive for." Then she burst into tears and said, "I committed many sins, and I pray every day facing the River Liffey so that my sins will drown in the river and I can again be as innocent as the day I was born."

I stood up and threw myself on the bed. I was burning with desire and she was sitting in front of me. I tried to hide the way I felt.

But she was indifferent. She looked strong but impassive.

She got up and stood next to the fireplace.

159

"You can tell how I feel from the way I look," I said.

"The body is still your god, whereas I've gone beyond that since I discovered Christ."

I hated her control, her strength, and I thought, "She's a hypocrite or pretentious."

I decided to forget my body, if only temporarily, and I went to church with her.

When we went into the church, the mass had just begun. She sat down next to me in reverential mode. She was in awe of the words being intoned. After a while the congregation started to repeat some of the prayers after the priest. Then she passed me a piece of paper with the Psalms printed on it. I began to read but I had trouble keeping in time with the general rhythm of the hymns. Then I started to pick out her voice and follow that. In the end, my voice was in harmony with the others singing in the church. When the hymns were over, a woman stepped up to the microphone and started to tell the story of how she had come to find faith. She said that in the beginning she didn't believe in anything.

"Yes, I didn't believe," she said. "Here I am before you, full of confidence and strength, not the strength of pride, but of humility, of submission to the power of knowledge, and faith in God and in Christ. A year ago I stood among you as a lost woman, brokenhearted after an unsuccessful affair with a man who exploited my childishness and my girlish innocence. The result was an unwanted pregnancy that I ended. The fetus, wrapped in cotton wool, was thrown onto the bank of the River Liffey. That night I saw hungry rats gnawing on its limbs. I was a wretched woman, begging for the affection and attentions of men and throwing herself into the arms of strangers every night. My father abandoned me when I was a young girl and moved to the United States. Then he worked as a mercenary in the Gulf War. My mother was addicted to alcohol and to men. Years of neglect and aimlessness, until a day came when I took some pills a boyfriend offered me before having sex and I went into a coma and was taken to the nearest hospital. When I opened my eyes, a nurse called Rose was the light that entered my heart.

She stood by my side and guided me to the path of true faith, and I discovered the purity of faith, and I discovered the cleanliness and purity of the Virgin and her love for those who have been cleansed.

"If I were destined to die today, and I met my Lord and ascended to the Kingdom of Heaven, then the righteous angels would receive me. And if that didn't happen, it would suffice me that Christ had cleansed me and had anointed my brow with water and oil." Tears streamed down her face. She allowed the entire congregation to see them. Everyone applauded her until she melted into the crowd.

Suddenly I imagined myself in the shoes of one of the people who had come to confess in public in a moment of honesty and catharsis. But what would I tell them? I would tell them that I was here studying for a doctorate, as I always liked to say, with pride and confidence, or I would say that I was here wavering between the truth and a mirage, between reality and dreams, between belief and disbelief, between chastity and filth and sin, between suppressed desires and a desire that could not possibly be fulfilled, and escaping the shackles of my body and of class. What would I say? Poor and needy, but there is a dream I want to fulfill.

I would say that I'm falling into the abyss of "not-self" and I suffer from a split personality and from a sense of perpetual, inexplicable oppression. I would say that all the choices I make are wrong and that I haven't understood who I am. Why me? I would say that I'm a victim of myself, of my family, of my environment, of my country, which is groaning under the weight of incompetence and many other problems. I would say that I'm a genius who suffers from bouts of madness and frustration, that sometimes I can't tell the difference between what's right and what's wrong. I would say that history has been unfair to me, and my body has been unfair to me, and the color of my skin has caused me grief. And my language is an obstacle and an impregnable barrier between myself and others! I would say that I'm afraid and nervous and on guard, and I have worries and misgivings and fantasies, and that I can't forget my body or shut down my mental processes. Or should I confess that I'm possessed by some other person who wants to scream and weep in public, to lament his own tragedy and the tragedy of all

161

humanity? I would state that I have been close to madness and to nonexistence. And I might break down and say that I'm a small boy who was destined to live again when he fell from the window of his house because the girl next door was passing him her doll from the window opposite, and that I fell on my head, and broke my arm and my spine, and I was miraculously saved after a coma that lasted a whole month, and that I feel that the boy died and didn't come around again and didn't come back to life and that it's the boy's soul that grows and moves and gets larger, and it's become a soul called Moataz. I am Moataz, a soul, not a body or a being. Just ether, a product of the memories of his parents and his brothers out of what Moataz would have been if he had been destined to live, just as they imagine their brother Hussein to be—if he had been destined to live. Of course they would have liked him to be an excellent student, to obey his parents, and to serve his country, sacrificing himself for its sake and for the sake of others, to graduate from university and get a teaching job. Perhaps he would become a head of department or a dean or a minister who would give his family a place in the history of Egypt and among its rulers. Or perhaps an Azhar scholar as his grandfather had hoped his father would be, though his father had dismally failed to fulfill the grandfather's prediction. He had learned the Qur'an by heart, but was a long way from interpreting or explaining it. So he would tell them he was a spirit, a spirit inspired by God! But isn't that rather hard to believe?! So he wouldn't confess.

Chapter 34

I saw Frida one Saturday night with Rebecca and her husband, as she came back from the bar. I was selling flowers outside the Zanzibar. She was walking along Bachelors Walk, and I was surprised at the way she looked. She had changed into another person. She seemed to be drunk and was saying and doing strange things. She looked rather trashy; that was obvious from her tight clothes, which did not suit her age, and her choice of colors. Rebecca, on the other hand, was pretending to be a lady, walking arm in arm with her husband at a leisurely pace. Suddenly Frida made some acrobatic moves in the street, stood on her hands like a gymnast, and threw her lithe body at my chest and thighs, groping my private parts with her hands, kissing me on the face, and clinging to me like a lover or someone desperate for sex. I took her in my arms; she was laughing aloud and saying, "We're the lords of the world," and then chanting "Allahu akbar, allahu akbar" hysterically. Then she screamed and swayed and said, "Tell your Lord to find a solution for Frida."

I saw her walk away, past the Four Courts Building with unsteady steps on her way to her house in the Northside. I was worried a speeding car might hit her. She crossed the road and the River Liffey was now behind her. Rebecca's sadness, the sadness of the people of Dublin, and my sadness were reflected in the pale lights and in the river water.

I was carrying a bunch of flowers. I crossed the Ha'penny Bridge to Temple Bar to sell the flowers. It was past one o'clock in the morning and it was time for the customers to come out of the Zanzibar on Ormond Quay, and from the Duke, the Turk's Head, the Kitchen, Sinners, the Front Lounge, and the Oak.

I didn't avoid the Front Lounge as I had done with the George, because I wanted people to buy the flowers I was carrying. Every flower meant an Irish pound, and every pound meant staying longer, and more books for research. The men in the Front Lounge were cultured and physically fit. They wore tight trousers and looked at me. "It's a pity you have to beg," one of them told me.

"A flower selling flowers," said another, "Throw the flowers away and kiss me and I'll give you fifty pounds." I spat in his face and he laughed campily.

Another one invited me to a drink in the bar. I hesitated. At the end of the night he offered to drive me home, but I thanked him and declined. Some of them were writers and poets, because I had seen them before in the Irish Writers' Union, and some of them were artists whose pictures I had seen in the Irish Film Centre. When I felt bored, I left the Front Lounge. I went to the Kitchen club because the young people there would buy flowers without asking the price and would leave a generous tip. They would take the opportunity to give the flowers to their girlfriends, and the flowers would open the door to love, and a path to the opening of lips and to kissing. I would turn my face away for fear of temptation. I used to pray often and ask for forgiveness, and daydream in front of the fire in my room and remember Hell and try to rise above temptation. But I was always certain that I was doing only the right thing—seeking knowledge, that is, regardless of the means.

Chapter 35

Moataz, you don't know what you want.

You have to know yourself first. You have to ask yourself who you are. What's your essence? Your nature? It's imperative that you define what you want and what you are doing in your life. That you search for your identity to know who you are. Isn't that the secret that nature placed in mankind since he was first formed from a drop of sperm in his mother's womb? The puzzling code of humanity. Then he told himself, "You're not King Oedipus to solve the riddle of humanity and then to be cursed for ever."

Do I want the body or the spirit? Do you want to surrender completely to Simone and live with her in sin, or do you want to stay chaste?

If I want the body, will the spirit's desire to know more fade away? How can I let go physically when I have such a long history of taboos and conventions that inhibit the body's wild impulses? Then there's the spirit, mysticism, asceticism, the desire to merge with the elements of the universe, then the sharpness of vision, then the insight, then the perspicacity, then union with the creator, for you to be the hand with which He strikes, and to be His word, with which you tell the thing to be, and it is.

Moataz, you're greedy. You want to be a demigod. Or rather you want to be Christ, you want to be one with God, to be the hand with which He strikes and the tongue with which He speaks, to have your iron vision look inside people's hearts and see the unknown.

Frida hadn't been out to work for more than ten days. I asked the toothless woman who sold newspapers and fruit next to the McDonald's in O'Connell Street about her. "She's confined to bed and won't be coming," she said. She spoke to me with an anxious look in her eyes. I looked at the way her mouth moved when she spoke, and I remembered what Frida had said about why this woman's teeth had fallen out—that she loved oral sex. I felt disgusted but I laughed. Next to her there was another old woman of about seventy, struggling to make a living. She sold fruit all year round and at Christmastime she sold firecrackers and other fireworks for children. I asked her about Frida and if she could give me her address, and she did so.

Her husband wasn't at home. She was pale and thin. She annoyed me. She refused to have any tea. She thanked me for taking an interest in her and asking after her. I wanted to leave but she assured me her husband wouldn't be back now for some time. They had argued and he had gone to the bar to drink. "He'll come back," I said. "He's exploiting you. He doesn't really love you. You're just a source of money, no more and no less."

She dismissed the idea and said, "I love him. That's the tragedy."

Enraged, I said, "Break free. You have to be brave."

She said, "You're still young and you have no experience of love. I fell in love with him. I live with him although I'm married to another man. I have a daughter by him and now I'm pregnant again and that's why I'm so thin. The doctor told me the pregnancy could be a danger to my life and I should abort it. My man is against abortion and insists I should have his child, and in Ireland the government also bans abortion."

"Having a child means more welfare from the Irish government," I said, "and more welfare means more drink, and more drink means your boyfriend will sleep with more Irish women. The English are always like that, destructive and exploitative."

She didn't respond to my prejudiced outburst, which I know had no basis in fact and was just personal impressions linked to my

166

unease about this man, no more and no less, and to my sympathy for Frida and the state she was in.

"Look after your health," I said, "and if you want any money, don't worry."

"Thank you," she replied. "God bless you. You've comforted me with this visit. Don't worry, I'll go back to work and wrap flowers for you as I've always done." She paused a while, then said, "I don't think Rebecca will be going out either."

"You're tougher than Rebecca," I said. "Rebecca's busy with her children and her husband."

"I think she wants another child with him," she said with a laugh.

"Very well then," I said, and she laughed.

I took my leave. I went down the stairs. I looked up and found her standing on the landing looking down at me, a look of sadness and farewell in her eyes. I felt sick at heart.

Chapter 36

I regretted leaving Edna's house, because I felt at home there and I realized how gentle and kind she was. I hadn't understood her behavior from the start: she was single, even if she did have children, and she wanted to live a free life, and when her children grew up they had to be independent, though if they needed her, her house was open to them.

I missed the trees around Edna's house, which I felt protected me from evil spirits and from loneliness and homesickness. I missed the bar where the kind woman worked. I used to visit it whenever I'd finished work or university every evening so that her smile and her pure spirit would put my mind at ease.

I bought flowers from Frida and Rebecca weekly and kept them somewhere cold, especially when winter came to stay as an unwelcome visitor, because they no longer went out as much as they did in summer, when I would buy flowers day by day. The last time I met Frida was a Saturday and she was standing on O'Connell Bridge arranging her flowers, with the River Liffey like a lake of frozen gray, the wind blowing in all directions and the sky mizzling as usual. I imagined she had come from frozen Hell. Frida was wearing a yellow tracksuit that matched the color of her skin and her exhausted face. She was wiping the rainwater off her face. I offered her my umbrella to protect her, but she refused, arguing that she was used to the weather, but I insisted on giving it to her.

"We men are tougher than you women," I said.

But she rejected my remark and said that's what our illusions suggest to us, because women are much stronger than men, but it's men, by brute force and with their long history of enslaving women, that have imposed these ideas. I was surprised by how aware this simple woman was when she spoke. I said, "There are many women in the Middle East who never think about the oppression they face and don't ask why the suffocating traditions behind the way men treat them have existed since time immemorial."

I sat alone in my little room in Nelson Street in Dublin's Northside. A modest room with a fire, a bookcase above it on which I put my books, a bed that hugged the wall under a high window without curtains, showing blue sky and the tall tower of the church, where birds had nested that had become my friends in my loneliness, a shower stall at the bottom edge of the bed, an electric stove, and a wash basin on another side of the room. The long hours passed and the color of the sky changed from blue to black. The moon wasn't visible in the cloudy sky and the birds had disappeared, only to reappear in the morning.

I sit and write poems that smell of nostalgia and a sense of exile. I write "Siham" in hundreds of poems without metre. They would work as prose poems in a collection of adolescent writings like the writings of the Locust Group, coming out in an irregular publication such as *The Other Writing*.

Outside the room runs a long, narrow corridor that leads to the other floors in the building. On the second floor live a young Tunisian and his Pakistani girlfriend. At first I thought she was Indian but when I met her in Moore Street Market once she told me she was a Pakistani brought up in England. This was clear from her perfect English accent. Her family had moved to London after the partition of India, and she had fallen in love with this Tunisian man and traveled to Ireland with him. Because they were recently married, I gave them some lilies and they were delighted. They promised to invite me to dinner with them, but it never happened.

In the apartment above them lived the Moroccan man who had shown me the house, along with his brother.

The beautiful Irish woman, who I thought was American at first, and who looked like a Hollywood actress, with her dark blue eyes, her beautiful complexion, and her carefully tailored clothes, lived on the very top floor.

I was always waiting for her to turn up. When I heard the door opening, I would rush into the corridor in the hope of finding her so that I could exchange a few words with her.

Once when she wanted to make a call, I pretended I was speaking on the phone, and I took the opportunity to get to know her better. She told me she was studying at Trinity College and she was surprised that I was also studying there. She said she had seen me in the library several times, but when she unexpectedly saw me outside the Zanzibar selling flowers she hadn't spoken to me, and the look in her eyes suggested she was puzzled. "Are you a flower seller or an exchange student?" she asked.

The trials and tribulations of living in exile make me long for home. I have a dream about going back to Cairo. I'm delighted at first but when I meet my sister at the airport I feel sad. Why haven't I finished my mission in Dublin? I ask the airport worker, "Aren't there any flights to Dublin now?" He looks at my ticket and says indignantly, "This is just a one-way ticket to Cairo, not a return. You'll have to buy another ticket to go back to Dublin." I look in my pocket. No money and no passport. I only find one bag and when I go up to it to pick it up, it changes into a shroud. Frightened, I call out to some of the people around me to carry the shroud to the grave but no one answers me.

I wake up sad. I open my eyes and find the church tower with just a few birds defying the cold air, but they soon move off to their nests, where it's warm and they can cuddle up with their loved ones.

I leave my room and call Siham in Cairo, without telling her who I am. I just listen to her voice and go back to my room. I think of washing my clothes. I pick up the clothes basket and put the clothes in the washing machine. I meet the young man who lives next door

170

with his friend. He avoids looking me in the eye, although I'm not accusing him of anything. When his friend sees him, he tells him to come in. I didn't try to ask about that look, but I realized he was jealous, since he wouldn't let him go out alone for even a minute. Even when they get home he wouldn't go to the door of the building unless they were together. I don't care about him: it's just curiosity to find out about others that makes me interested. The young Tunisian, the husband of the Pakistani woman, said, "If they don't leave this building, it's bound to collapse on us as God did with Sodom and Gomorrah, because God doesn't like a house inhabited by sinners."

Once I told him, "We're not in Algeria or Cairo. This is their country, and God will prove you wrong, because we're good people and we live in the same building, and God isn't so unfair that he would destroy us all indiscriminately."

Chapter 37

The woman who lives in the basement told me that the two men have been living together since she moved into the building. She has a grudge against one of them because he's in the habit of stealing the underwear she leaves in the washing machine. I imagined the scene as a farce, with the man putting on woman's clothing. This neighbor is married to an African whose nationality I don't know, but I think he's from Zambia. At first, I was frightened of the way he looked at me when he stood next to the door talking on the phone. He didn't have a telephone in his room so he made his calls in the hallway, where there was a phone. He spoke English with an African accent. I didn't like his loud voice. I often wanted to open the door of my room and tell him to lower his voice, but I would hesitate and say to myself, "He's got both you and the Irish to contend with." And sometimes I would say. "He's African and a kinsman of ours. Don't judge people by their skin. Calm down." That's how I spoke to myself to suppress my anger and reconsider my concept of being foreign.

I went into the café carrying my flowers, not knowing what to do with them. I had failed to meet Frida, and I was aware of the value of what she was doing for my sake. That's how I always am, appreciating women after they have slipped away from me, feeling their presence only when I lose them. Are all men like that, I wonder?

Perhaps this was the main reason why a woman leaves a man after the man fails to control her. At first she makes threats, and he doesn't take any notice. Then he says, "It's just women's threats." Then the woman changes, then she disappears completely and manages to run away and soar far out of his sight.

The smell of coffee and chocolate filled the place. All the customers in the café picked up their drinks and put them on the tables.

The sight of sausages disgusted me and the smell of them annoyed me. The warmth of the place and the music coming from the corners of the café made me feel morose and languid. Some lovers were sitting close to me. Why am I alone like this, I wondered. Why do I avoid experimenting?

I ran away from Siham and didn't defend my love.

I ran away from Simone and didn't continue with her.

Now I'm a man drowning in disappointments and nostalgia.

The singer's voice, sobbing and lamenting her lover who was gone, reminded me of my own situation.

To die is to part.
To meet is to be born.
And these candles that mourn your absence
Are also your shining light
The day you return.
So come back soon before I melt
And the world goes dark.

To hear sad music, to walk in the rain, to have premonitions of an early death, to be afraid that love might slip away from you and abandon those who love you, to be jealous and not to say so openly, to go to lonely and deserted places.

These are love. These are the signs that you are romantic.

My Moroccan neighbor Adnan often knocks on my door. He likes to come by and sit with me. Once he cried in my room while listening to the Cheb Khaled song "Wahran." He said, "My mother's been waiting for me since I left and I don't know if she's still alive. Now's the time for the grape harvest and I think she'll be keeping my share till I go back." I remembered my own mother, who said, "I'll keep your share of the mangoes in the fridge."

"All mothers are kind," I told him. "You'll go back and find her waiting, maybe carrying a bunch of grapes."

He wiped his tears away and laughed. I complained that I had pains in my back and legs from standing outside bars to sell flowers.

"Wait," he said.

He went out, then came back in a while carrying a bottle.

"This olive oil will cure you if you rub it into your skin. It has the light and spirit of God in it."

He began to oil my neck with it. I succumbed to the movement of his strong fingertips and to the light of the Lord.

Rebecca and Frida went on a cruise around the Mediterranean, including Turkey and Israel and ending in Sinai. They were very much looking forward to the trip. They said they wanted to see the world and find out about geography, antiquities, and the way other people live. Rebecca said that if she had finished her education she would have been a geography teacher. "Isn't it beautiful to draw maps of the world, reducing the world to lines and points?" she said. A few days before she left she smiled and blew me a kiss. In a voice that was affectionate and flirtatious she said she wanted to borrow some money, because she wanted to finish off the arrangements for the trip, and she also wanted to buy some things in Istanbul for her children, so she was reluctant to speak to me openly and was afraid I wouldn't lend her the money. But I agreed in the end because I had borrowed some money from them to buy flowers and hadn't paid it back. I said, "And how's Frida going to fly when she's pregnant?" and she answered, "She's in her final months so there's nothing to worry about. And anyway, if she loses the baby it'd be good. We don't want any more English in our country."

I missed her greatly and I had to buy flowers from other traders, and it wasn't the same dealing with them. When she came back Rebecca said she really loved Sharm el Sheikh because the water was so clear, the service was excellent, and you really felt it was a land where prophets had walked. She mentioned Moses often.

Then she said, "Egyptian men are very courteous and they treat women with respect." Then she headed toward the Liffey and said, "If I wasn't married I would have stayed there a long time." Then she talked about the cleaning man she became attached to. Sometimes she refused to go to the sea so that she could exchange a few sentences with him. She deliberately tempted him so that she could feel how aroused he was. Two hours before she left, while Frida was on the beach, she almost made love with him, had not the feeling that she was betraying her husband prevented consummation of the act, and she left him in the lurch.

She said that she never imagined that Egypt was so beautiful, and so free that women could go topless in front of men on the beach, and that she pitied the men. Then she said, "In the evening I watched the moon on the sea as it kissed the waves, and I almost believed that they were lovers." And she said, "Lord forgive me, but when I'm in the open air or in the desert or by the sea, I feel completely primitive. I feel that it's my instincts that are driving me. There was nothing special about the cleaning man except that he was a man who desired me. And I deliberately aroused him. When he was cleaning the room, the air conditioning wasn't working properly so I asked him to check it, and I deliberately stood very close to him. Then he began looking at me and with my feminine instinct I knew that he wanted me, and that's what I wanted too. But I resisted him till the end." Then she paused. "A married woman has to keep her sacred vow and show some modesty," she added.

"Obviously, that's really sacred!" I said.

Frida interrupted. "Her luck's always like that. She falls for the right man. But me, I always meet bastards. That Italian was good for nothing but dancing and talking about the art exhibitions he'd seen all over the world, but he'd come to Egypt specially to see the Fayoum portraits, which were going to be shown in a special exhibition in Sharm el Sheikh." She added that he didn't kiss her even on the forehead, he had a special interest in bodies and in nakedness, in both men or women, and that he could determine people's

175

mental health by looking at their chests and legs. Rebecca said she very much hated Istanbul and was surprised how many mosques and minarets there were, and she began to imitate the call to prayer: "Allahu akbar, Allahu akbar." "There are more Muslims than Christians," she said. "I hated the many bazaars that had everything, from spices to mobile phones. It's a big market." A Turkish man harassed her in one shop. He closed the door on her and started to kiss her, but Frida saved her at the last minute. She completely hated Tel Aviv and couldn't understand why there were so many tanks on the streets. The people there looked miserable and she felt frightened of them. Nobody smiled at her, and wherever she went she saw armed men, and there were always ambulances rushing down the street. I didn't have the time or the energy to explain the Arab–Israeli conflict to her in detail or tell her that Israel was a state at war and ready for war, that it wants to get its revenge on those who organized the Holocaust, and it wants a homeland, even if it costs seas of blood and comes about at the expense of the Palestinians. Frida asked, "Where's Palestine on the map? Is it in Europe?"

The Tears of Heaven

Chapter 38

He did not wear his scarlet coat,
For blood and wine are red,
And blood and wine were on his hands
When they found him with the dead,
The poor dead woman whom he loved,
And murdered in her bed.
Oscar Wilde, *The Ballad of Reading Gaol*

Frida went and never came back. They said she had died having an abortion. She had died to gratify the mistaken beliefs of other people. She was dreaming of another child and then this child was conceived through love, her love for that Englishman. She didn't love her Irish husband. I remembered her putting her hand on her stomach and looking at the River Liffey, after Rebecca referred to the fact that she was living in sin with a man other than her husband. For the first time, her tears mixed with the waters of that ancient and eternal river, which preserved the sorrows and joys of the people who had crossed the river, next to which she stood selling her flowers, and the smell of which she never liked. This silent angel that the world enjoyed mistreating, this poor flower seller, always pursued by the police, from her childhood through her youth. She had left two girls and a young son. I imagined her younger daughter crying for her at night and the morning after her mother's death her grandmother would tell her not to go to school that day and to take off her uniform and go to the market to buy flowers to sell to lovers in the evening. She would go, willingly and unwillingly, because it wouldn't make any compelling difference to the passers-by or the customers that a girl was lost, that a dream had been shattered, and innocence had died: because she was now an orphan.

As she left for Omagh, Simone said her trip, and the singing by her group, was an opportunity to say that the world can be brought together by love rather than war, that peace sows the seeds of happiness for this world, that her group is the best proof of that, and that art can solve all crises, even disputes over land. I said, "Don't go. The North is a dangerous place." "Don't worry," she said. "I'm going to live a long life." Then she started to recall incidents when she had almost lost her life: how she had fallen in the water when playing alone on a small bridge between the banks of a canal in her village in Wicklow when she was two, and again when she slipped on a stage when performing a dance step and had to lie on her back for a whole month, and how she almost died a third time when she fell off her bicycle going down a hill on a rainy night and how she miraculously survived. She said her faith in what she was doing would make sure she survived.

The train station wasn't crowded—just a few passengers and the members of her group. The English woman with the curly hair threw a cold look, and the effect on Simone was evident. "Filthy bitch," she muttered. But she forgot about it when I went right up to her and she hugged and kissed me. Then she rushed toward the train, looking over her shoulder. When she disappeared I felt empty, tired, and hopeless—a feeling I often have after I leave a woman. And sometimes I have a feeling of nostalgia and frustration. I was most uncertain how to interpret it, and when it started to recur I decided to reduce the time I spent among women.

The head of the department said, "We can't extend your research visit any longer than this. The dean has refused. He said, 'He's come to sell flowers, he argues with the local people, forges our banknotes, and goes out with our women. No doubt he'll tarnish our image in what he writes when he goes back. This creature didn't come here to do research but to loaf around to find material for his novels.'" Then she said with emotion, "I think it's enough. I hope you've fulfilled your objective from this visit to our country. I know you've had a very hard time but it was your choice from the beginning. If I had been in your place I couldn't have put up with the hardship and the risks. Thank God you've survived physically, and I hope you'll learn from your mistakes." Then she lowered her voice a little, almost to a whisper. "Your life here has been a big mystery. You'll be free to talk about it if you want one day, but you should know that we liked you and we've given you a chance." Suddenly as she spoke I remembered her son on my first visit to her house, when he spoke about the genie that lives in the Irish hills and I wondered whether the genie had brought me happiness or misery. I felt dizzy and almost fell over. I went on to tell her that it was unfair, that I hadn't finished my research yet, I'd be disappointed if I had to go home and abandon my studies, and it didn't matter whether I suffered or not. What mattered was to fulfill my dream and the dream of my family and my teachers. But she was determined to convey the university's message to me. I found out later that it was Sari who had told the university about my work and the forgery incident, maybe to get revenge on Simone and possibly on me.

A dream

They arrested me at home.

They said, "You've come to kill our women and violate our honor." Then they handcuffed me.

And they blindfolded me.

They put me on a bus and forced me to sit down.

I resisted their cold cruel hands.

When I went into the police station, they said, "Why did you kill the woman who sold flowers, the poor woman? Did you rob her? Did you hate her that much? Or were you worried that your illicit relationship with her might come to light? Why did you kill her?"

She was a poor woman who wanted to bring up her sick daughter, who needed a blood transfusion every six months.

I said, "I didn't kill her. You killed her with your cruelty, your meanness toward her, and your negligence. I didn't kill her. Maybe her English boyfriend killed her, the one who got money out of her and cheated on her all the time he lived with her, or maybe her ex-husband killed her, but I didn't kill her, I didn't kill her.

"I loved her."

Chapter 39

Omagh, 1998

It was like the Day of Judgment, with people rising from the dead! Voices shouting. I saw it on television: mangled flesh and the bodies of children, women, old men, and youths. The camera focused on a pair of shoes stained in blood, the face of a girl bleeding, with her burnt doll by her side, a severed foot lying next to a young man. Why do people kill each other? Why do we thirst to destroy each other? Why does the myth of Cain and Abel play out again and again across the world? If it's not killing with knives, it's with looks or words, or with dynamite. How many assassinations are carried out through words? What's happening in Palestine is the same as what happened in Europe: the laughs turn into screams. How many beautiful bodies change into body parts and corpses? They said the Real IRA was behind this act. Is that true?

Is this terrorism, or honorable defense of country and territory? Fighting for survival. The IRA defends its right to a sovereign Irish state and to put an end to English power and domination. Will a bomb in a bus, or a supermarket, or in front of a school, or a church, or a mosque, intimidate the occupier? The Palestinians do that to liberate Jerusalem and set up a secure homeland for themselves. Hamas, Hezbollah, and the Aqsa Martyrs Brigades recognize martyrdom for the sake of the country, and say it's better for one person to die a martyr than for a whole nation to die. Terrorism or honorable defense of the country! There's no theater of war, no front line, so let it be guerrilla warfare. The occupiers have a moral position on martyrdom. By their own logic they don't recognize it and they see it as terrorism. But the occupied have a different position because they are losing hope in dialogue, so let there be violence. But what have they done wrong, these innocent children, these old men, women, and youths? What have they done wrong, the occupied who are hungry, sick, and humiliated? Confusing, isn't it?

Chapter 40

Simone was killed in a terrorist attack in Omagh in Northern Ireland, in County Tyrone, when a car bomb blew up. It had been planted by the Real IRA, which objected to the IRA's decision to accept the Good Friday Agreement. She died with 28 others.

She paid the price for her love of peace. She died betrayed. Her blood spilled on ground that had not known peace since the English set foot on it, and she died in the Royal Victoria Hospital.

I was told about it by her friend Laura, who was working in the Meath Hospital in Dublin, and whom I had met more than once, in the singing group and also in the Irish Film Institute. As tears rolled down her cheeks, she said, "The explosion took place in Lower Market Street. She was there after the performance. She had gone to the shops to buy some accessories for the group, such as clothes decorated with silk and satin for the women to wear during the performance when they were to sing the song you taught them, "Henna, henna, O drop of dew." She had wanted the girls to look like djinn from *A Thousand and One Nights*. She had wanted to honor you with an oriental tableau."

Then she paused. "The explosion severed one of her arteries," she continued between sobs, "and she bled a lot." She took a package out of her handbag and and handed it to me, saying, "Simone told me to give you this if I saw you. It's your birthday present.

When she found you ignoring her in recent times she decided to send it to you through me because she was too embarrassed to meet you while you were working." When I opened the present it was a book of Irish folk songs with a CD, and a card with hearts bleeding, along with a message.

In it she said, "Remember me forever. I tried every possible way to make you happy, but you always held me off, as if your emotions were imprisoned inside you, but that doesn't matter. I will always love you. I know you'll say I've created inside you a sadness as big as the world but I'm not wholly responsible for that. I tried to love you, and I'm not sure whether you loved me or not! But you are very important in my life, even if we didn't exchange kisses or make love regularly. It's enough to be with you. It's enough to look in your eyes and feel the warmth of your hands. Don't forget me. I know you'll go back to Cairo and I know you'll miss me. I know that one day you'll write about me or come to Dublin to look for me. Maybe you'll find me, or maybe I'll be with some African tribe, or in some American state, but the only certainty I have is that I'll miss you, and perhaps you will remember me. I'm well aware that each of us is looking for love, and when we find it we will hang on to it, even if it's a dream, and even if we lose it. We pledge ourselves to this love for years and years and the love and the beloved might abandon us, but we will remain attached to it. There is first love and unrequited love, and we always prefer these two kinds of love because they represent an ideal, an elevated concept of love, just like the idea of man's devotion to God. An eternal, fundamental idea in the life of mankind, and even if some deny His existence they continue to remember and grieve for the time when they were close to God and for the comfort provided by the faith that is now lost.

"I know that you stand by this idealistic form of love, just as you hold on to the idea of faith, because you do really love, and really believe."

Why did she go there? Why did she die? Why didn't I prevent her from going?

Why her in particular? I killed her. I could have said to her, "Don't go." And she would have agreed and deferred to my wishes as she always did. Why did they kill her? She didn't do anything. She didn't take part in a demonstration, and she had never protested in her life.

A singer who loved art and peace! She had left her boyfriend because he liked violence and was a killer, and she loved me because I was a writer and peaceful. It was I who handed her over to them, it was I who took part in this mass slaughter, I who forced her to go and to die. I'm the murderer. Why didn't I reciprocate her love? Why wasn't I kind to her? I was arrogant, saying, "She's a country girl, a liberated woman." And I lived in the delusion that I loved Siham. Do you think that's chivalry? Is that manliness? I doubt it. You're a coward, frightened, tense, and mad. You're hesitant, and he who hesitates is neither a man nor a human.

You read Thomas Mann's *Death in Venice* and are surprised at the fate of the hero. You shudder to think of meeting the same end and dying that way in Dublin and being buried in this foreign land, your body merging with this cold soil, under constant rains and snows, where your body would miss the heat of the soil of the Nile and the warmth of the Theban sun, which preserves bodies for eternity.

Those who die abroad die alone, and those who live abroad die a thousand times. That's what I read in the classics. The bodies of those who die in foreign lands are exempt from Hell, whatever sins they have committed. How wonderful those hadiths are, the ones recounted, of course, by those who collected hadiths! Of course, they weren't people from Mecca or Medina, but from Byzantium, Persia, and Asia, where missing one's country and being far from home meant pure death and exile.

Departure.

Does love kill? And are those who die of it also martyrs?

He picks up his heavy suitcases, heavy as the sins of all mankind. There are no perfumes or new clothes in them, just many books with strange letters that neither his father nor mother will read, nor even his sisters. He picks them up like a giant rock that makes him bend double. No one offers to lend him a hand, though a few old women look at him sympathetically and apologize that they cannot help him.

Darkness fell and it rained. The air was saturated with water vapor. The mist was like a window through which he looked out on the world. The buildings of Trinity College looked like fortresses on which mythical birds had nested and in whose towers Dracula appeared with his flashing eyes and his fangs. Rain poured down and the wind blew and he thought it was a hurricane and he looked for the ship and couldn't find it. His eyes began to wander, unable to focus on anything. In succession he saw or imagined: his first nights after arriving in Dublin, the houses he had lived in and was evicted from, the friends and kindhearted people he had met: Simone, Edna, Frida, Mario, Rebecca, Abu Alam, the head of the department, Joanna. All of them paraded in front of him.

And suddenly the darkness became the long road on which he was embarking. Thick smoke surrounded him. From afar he heard the sound of a plane roaring, so he headed to the airport with frightened, hesitant steps.

You lived alone there in faraway lands and the wind almost blew you into the sea, where the waves would have swept you away. The sun never rose. You heard the sound of the waves crashing on the surface of the raging sea, and you were scared. You walked and walked, gripped by fear. Your arms and legs trembled from loneliness and cold. Tears fell from your eyes like a stray child who had lost the elder sister who was holding his hand a few moments earlier, and then went off to get him some candy from the store nearby. Then suddenly he found himself alone except for his memory and the fear of loss.

Why leave? Why did you hate Dublin, the climate there, the rain, and the people? Why did you leave the trees to themselves and the streets wet? Why did you leave the genies on the windows and the monks in the monasteries? Why did you leave the churches, the mosques, the temples, the bars, the flowers, the smell of coffee and tea, and the sugar cubes? Why did you leave the libraries and the antique books? Why did you leave the cozy winding streets? Why did you leave the castles, the mansions, and the curtains that hide secrets behind them? With the snows and the winds behind you, and the sun and the parched land in front of you, why were you afraid of loneliness? Why were you weary of freedom? Was homesickness a specter that would swallow you up and kill you? So you ran away and saved yourself, or you were afraid to die in a cheap room in some old building on a bed stained with the sweat and other body fluids of feverish nights and tawdry sex? You hadn't finished writing your dissertation, but you decided to leave anyway. You said, "I'll save myself and throw the rock off my shoulders. I won't go down the mountain to pick it up as Sisyphus did in the ancient Greek legend." You gathered your things together at speed. You bought a suitcase as big as Noah's ark, and put all your books and old, worn-out clothes in it. You didn't buy gifts for anyone, and you said, "I'm going to leave immediately." You paid the electricity bill and the rent, and you didn't say goodbye to your Irish neighbor or the Moroccan or the two young men who lived next door to you in the building.

You ran off guiltily. You were afraid of losing yourself and God, or that your father would die when you were far away, especially after your sister told you that in your absence your father was at death's door every night and in a loud voice called out for you to come to him, as if you were Joseph and he were Jacob.

Three days at Dublin airport carrying your heavy bags full of books. The airline wanted a small fortune from you to carry them, and when you told them you were a research student, they told you that was your problem, and when you said you'd throw your books in the filthy Liffey, they cursed you and said, "Is that our reward for treating you so well? Is that a 'thank you' for us inviting you to our country? This is Ireland's fate, to receive only ingratitude and denial from its friends." But a woman who worked in the Aer Lingus office took pity on me and helped me check in my bags for a paltry amount: a box of chocolates was the key. She loved Egyptians because she had met a taxi driver on her visit to Egypt and for a short time he had given her life meaning and made her feel that she was a woman. So she saved you after three days on the floor at Dublin airport, when the police were about to arrest you for begging or perhaps for "acts of terrorism." So you're back, but not as you were when you left. Everyone noticed that and said, "He's gained learning but he's lost his mind."

Chapter 41

Cairo, 2005

Sameh, her ex-husband, told me, "Siham is an actress and she wants to play a variety of roles. Perhaps that's because of the multiple personality disorder she has and the existential angst she has to live with and the dualism that disrupts her life: body and soul, desire and creativity, an eternal conflict. Her demons divide her into multiple personalities."

He advised me not to think about her, because her preoccupation with herself prevented her from seeing anything but herself. She was in a state of spontaneous combustion and would vaporize as the days passed. "You misjudge her," I said.

Then, looking at me carefully, he said, "Your infatuation with her is blinding you to the truth and blocking your ears to everything but her whisperings. I think you're a narcissist like her."

What he says is true. I don't know why she comes to mind every time I meet a new woman! Her hair, her eyes staring into space. Despite the contact lenses she wears, she can't see me. Her unruly hair that rejects all attempts to style it. Her Cleopatra bearing. Everything about her comes to mind whenever I approach or try to court any woman.

During the conversation with him, I say to myself, "She's frightened of me. She doesn't want to submit, and I'm the same. We've left behind us a history of suffering and bungling."

Sameh sighed and said, "Thank God I'm rid of her. Siham suffers from paranoia and megalomania. I think she'd be a good case study for departments of psychoanalysis. Maybe if Freud was alive, he could devote a whole lecture to analyzing her." I said to myself, "He's a liar and a madman." What he said made me desire her more, and I said, "He's hurt, disheartened, vengeful."

Why do I run away from her? I was happy to have her as my muse. Do I only want her as a character for a novel, to summon up whenever I'm short of women in my writings? Am I abusing her by associating with her? Whenever she sees me with my friends, she runs away, avoids talking to me. More than once I've seen her talking to many people, especially men who are not at all like me. Sometimes she offers them her hand and her cheeks, whereas we have only shaken hands once. On that occasion her hand was warm and the physical contact sent such a shiver of desire right through me that I can still feel it now.

At that time, Siham was single, having divorced her first husband, who later became a friend of mine. I don't know why we became friends or what it was that brought us together. Perhaps so that I could hear about her from him. Perhaps I was exploiting him. Sometimes I hate myself for conniving in this game. He for his part relished talking about her and about her faults. I tried by cunning to detect whether he was still in love with her, but he always said that she had made his life hell and had prevented him from being creative in Cairo. He thought that people listened to her more, and sympathized with her more, because she was a beautiful woman who knew well how to appeal to people and win their sympathy. Didn't I tell you she was a smooth operator? Perhaps she's neurotic: one of my colleagues in the world of literature analyzed her personality after making an exhaustive study of her writings and her theatrical performances. He devoted a whole chapter of his book to analyzing the psychological tension in the roles she has played and he applied Freud's theories about sex to them, using Jung's theories on the "shadow aspects" of men and women as well. He concluded that her personality fluctuated between, on the one hand, trying to assert her personality as a woman by writing obsessively and ostentatiously about physical things and, on the other hand, wanting to assume the ego of a man, which would give her more independence, and control, and put a nail in the coffin of women's historic subjugation to men.

Sometimes I wondered why he was telling me such precise details of the secrets they shared. Why did he always try to knock her off the pedestal on which I had placed her? Perhaps he knew that I loved her. I wonder, was he jealous of me or of her? Did he regret marrying her? He would always sigh dolefully and say, "Sins never go unpunished." The carnal pleasure had borne fruit in the form of her pregnancy and this would tie him to Siham forever, through a child that bore his name and had the same expression in his eyes, while taking from Siham her body, her energies, and her nervous tension.

I won't find fault with you, Siham, because of your life and what you do with it.

You can put these men on or take them off, as you do with your clothes, whether fancy or trashy, because you're freer than the wind, which is at least controlled by the divine will.

I won't ask you for any commitments, because you're not a fact but a fear. You are fear incarnated in front of my eyes, and behind us there is a long history of disappointments, existential misunderstanding, and tensions through the endless years of life that we have lived together in this life or in another.

You have made me a laughingstock in the eyes of others, who think that unrequited love is characteristic of the weak. But is love just sex? Yes, the function of sex is to make us addicted to the presence of someone else, especially when our instinctive needs must be met, but I believe that the delicate, fragile feelings associated with the soul have a secret that is more important and grander.

Chapter 42

Cairo, two years later

Roaming the streets of Cairo after coming back from Dublin, you saw Siham. She was sitting in the Café Riche, with a cup of coffee in front of her and a copy of the literary weekly *Akhbar al-adab* and Kawabata's novella *The House of the Sleeping Beauties*. She was looking at the dark Nubian waiter so that he would come over and she could order another cup of coffee. When she saw you through the window, coming along the passageway that leads to the Zahrat al-Bustan coffee shop, she waved to you, and you went in. You took no notice of the looks that Magdi, the owner and faithful guardian of the café, gave you. You sat down and she looked at you. You, Moataz, were confused and frightened, and you hadn't slept for months. She asked how you were and about your writings, and she asked you for a copy of the monodrama *The Woman Jailer*, which you had written for her some time ago. With wandering eyes and a shaky voice, you said that she was your jailer. You asked her why she did that to you when she was well aware that you loved her, why she tormented you by ignoring you, and why she always went for the wrong men, men who were dangerous? Then you asked her about that journalist, the voice and mouthpiece of the ruling party, and about the new marriage, how could she go off with him and leave you? You hadn't done anything in life other than love her and remain loyal to her memory. Even in Ireland she was your aspiration, your path, the way to make your dream come true, as well as the blinker that prevented you from getting involved in loving any other women. Now you had come back to find her worshiping at the sanctuary and shrine of another man, where she recited hymns and prayers of intimate love, drunk and intoxicated on the nectar and the taste of his love. With your hands trembling and your heart racing, you said, "Surely you realize that I love you and am faithful to you, but I am poor and destitute, and embarrassed because of my upbringing and my shyness."

"He needs me more than you," she said. "He confessed his love to me and he showered me with sympathy and generosity when I was alone and confused. He lent me a hand and gave me a job I couldn't have dreamed of. He offered me a decent home after I was lost in the slums of Cairo, especially after the death of my first husband, who had been providing for my son, and after my family threw me out because I had disobeyed them and because they couldn't accept my lifestyle, which was provocative, at least as far as they were concerned. His weakness made me aware of my strength, and I put up with the idea of having a relationship with a man who couldn't live alone any longer. Don't think I'm an opportunist, but think I fell in love with him. I didn't understand the way you looked at me during that short period, and how would I have known that you were in love with me? He beat you to it, declared himself, and offered tokens of his love. As for you, maybe you started seeing me as your muse. I am flesh and blood, and I have desires that course through my body like the blood in my veins. Maybe I'm a terrestrial creature and not celestial like you. I think it's the nature of women. Can't you see that they give birth and populate the land?" Then she laughed and said the best proof was their monthly periods, which always remind them of their basic function: the family, that is.

"My pregnancy was unsettled because my mental and physical state had deteriorated: my hair had started to fall out and for many months I couldn't bear having food in my stomach. He didn't understand what was wrong with me, and he thought there was another man or perhaps I was bored with living with him. He abandoned his pride even more. He regaled me with presents and was very obliging toward me and my family. Yes, I often remembered you. Especially when I went through Maadi, I missed you very much. And I often laughed and said, 'He's living with the blonde women there, drowning in alcohol and freedom.' As you can see, I'm not happy now, and the way out is separation."

Then she sighed and tears were about to run down from the corners of her eyes. "I don't think you were ready to declare your love. I lied when I said I didn't understand the way you looked at me. I have intuition. The way you always admired me! But there was a moment when I felt that I wasn't the right woman for you and that you weren't ready to start a relationship and that you were closed in on yourself. I knew it would be difficult to get through to you. We women sense that in a man and that's what decides how close we get and how quickly we become attached to him. You know that I very often think of suicide and have thoughts of death, and I want to throw myself off the balcony of my house or in front of a speeding car. But when I look at the moon that you're always talking about, I feel optimistic. The moon has a magical effect on my mood, and in moments of darkness inside me I see a full moon shining, clinging to you. Of course you're not the best man or the strongest or the most manly. Don't get angry or be surprised and say: 'She's divorced and experienced.' But intuition and observing lecherous men have taught me much. But you're better with your soul and your gentleness, even your weakness, which is very much like my weakness. Your humanness makes you sacred in my eyes. He was never jealous of you, but he didn't understand you and he didn't know how spiritual our relationship was or that there was no physical element in it or absolutely any desire for physical contact. You're my identical twin much of the time, but I'll tell you something." She took a sip of her coffee and began to look at the dark lines of coffee grains in the cup as if she were reading someone's fortune. "You'd better start again with a new woman," she said gloomily, "and try to forget me. I'm not the woman who suits you or suits any man. I think my world is art or travel." She put her hand on his cold hands and suddenly Moataz didn't feel anything: a blurred image of great

195

writers, pictures of artists, tables, books on a desk covered in dust, cars driving down Talaat Harb Street, ashtrays, nausea, his heart beating faster, suffocation, then a resounding fall. He opened his eyes and the face of Magdi the owner was comforting him after he recovered from fainting. He advised him to rest at home a while and completely forget the woman he was sitting with.

Chapter 43

Moataz's wedding

In a black tuxedo, a white dress shirt, a tie, and a vest, and with a paper flower in the lapel of your jacket, you smile, spruce yourself up, and take up the groom's position outside the hairdresser's. You look very clean, dazzling white thanks to your stag night, when your friends came to visit and asked you to give yourself a thorough cleansing, so you got into the bathtub and sank into the warm water, poured vast amounts of Sunsilk shampoo and Herbal Essences shower gel over yourself. Then you started to scrub your body with the loofah in the belief that you were washing away your past and your old love for Siham. You shaved your pubic hair, after almost losing the sense that you were a man. Your friends walked in on you and were aghast at the sight of you naked. They laughed and said, "God help her. What will the poor woman do with that?" You told them off, ordered them out, and sprayed water on them.

Your mother had told you to get married. She said that she wanted to see you have offspring before she died, and that her family and the neighbors were criticizing her for the fact that you weren't yet married. "If Moataz doesn't get married," they said, "he'll either go mad or turn into a eunuch." So you agreed to marry Alya, a relative of yours. You hadn't seen her since she was a child. You met at the wedding of one of your relatives, and you liked her. She looked like

197

an Irish woman, beautiful and taller than you. She was slim and had an angelic, soft face, and eyes as green as the hills of Ireland, so you said, "Why not? It's good to do things properly, and new beginnings are always salutary."

Alya came out of the beauty salon looking like one of those princesses that escape in fairy tales, like Cinderella or Snow White or others. She was stunningly beautiful, very imposing and splendid. You chose her out of many women, or perhaps it was she who chose you. She was from the country and she said, "Your history doesn't matter, what matters is our present life together." And you said, "She's innocent and she doesn't have the experience of city girls." She was faithful in her love and in her devotion to you. But after a while, you felt bored and pained because you had married Alya to atone for your guilt in abandoning Simone for no clear reason and for failing, without explanation, to declare your love to Siham sooner. You were frightened, tense, and on edge. Everyone was delighted, and she held your arm to show she was proud of you and to give herself courage, but you were distracted and unsettled. You were thinking of things absent and things present, of Simone and Siham, of what would happen after the wedding. You wondered, "Who's this holding on to me? Who are these people around me? The wedding, yes, it was a wedding and an auspicious wedding procession. A kiss on the bride's forehead, a wedding ring, red sherbet drinks—the color of love and desire and the blood that stains the bridal sheet, the proof of virginity. A white dress fringed with lace draped across your lap like a fig leaf from Paradise, people dancing and cheering, jostling to have their picture taken next to the two of you.

Without understanding anything, you joined them in dancing, prancing like an acrobat and singing a tune with a rhythm completely different from that of the music, and you almost fainted. She went to dance with her friends and relatives and with other men while you looked on to take in what was happening. Marriage in less than a month. To be declared, love needs at least three months, the same time a fetus needs for a soul and life to seep in. Less than a month isn't enough to know anyone with anything close to certainty. The separation took place just as quickly as the acquaintanceship began, because after the desire ended, the fear, the loneliness, and the antipathy returned. You felt that you had jumped voluntarily into a well and that you were the scapegoat for a society you had tried to rebel against but had failed. But, Moataz, you decided to be Moataz again. You decided to separate and move away. You lived for the idea of art and writing. Alya didn't understand why you had separated, and she wasn't aware of the changes or complications inside you. She was simple, young, and innocent and she didn't understand you or the history that had made you, that had subdued you and disfigured you.

You turned off your cell phone and said you would look for another Siham or a woman like her, but Alya was not the woman you wanted. She didn't completely understand, like Simone and Siham, so she became more neurotic, more hysterical, and sadder. She said you didn't understand anything about women, and that she wasn't as young and innocent as you claimed. She too asked for a separation, and you didn't meet. She sent a representative, her father, to arrange her divorce and that went ahead. You went back to your old delusion, looking for your dream woman. It wasn't Siham exactly, but it was something else you couldn't find, and you broke down. . . . Everyone understood what had happened to you and you were the only one who couldn't see, as if you were under a curse or some powerful force had messed up your mind and what was inside you, and you had lost your way in your dreams and memories and your women. This happened after you came back, but you lost your sense of the cycles of the sun, the moon, and the earth, and got lost in a world of timelessness and nonexistence.

Chapter 44

The carriage of time glides along, garlanded with pride and modesty.
No one hears the wheels creaking, because people only hear what they want to
hear . . . but the carriage does not stop and the world is an unfaithful husband.
Naguib Mahfouz, *The Harafish*

Since you left Dublin and came back, you've been very restless, always tense. You hear ringings and whisperings in your ears and you concentrate on a single idea that obsesses you for many days: the idea that there's someone who's going to kill you. You're confused and you stare at nothing, you have wandering eyes that flash with madness, and you see letters that form strange, frightening words whenever you read a book or a newspaper. You've started to be afraid of letters when words were once your profession. You don't finish your conversations with those close to you or even with the outsiders that you love. You've started to be afraid of people. You never close your eyes to sleep, but stay awake for nights on end, and you can sleep for days on end as well. Your bed has become the woman you never leave. You have neglected your appearance; you've let your beard grow as if afraid of a razor blade touching your icy skin, terrified that a pair of scissors might touch your hair. You looked like one of the venerable Seven Sleepers of Ephesus, dead but alive. You have neglected your work and would have been fired if it hadn't been for the kindness of your friends and your boss. Wasn't it she who sent you on the trip? No writing, no newspapers, no friends, no relatives, no telephone calls, no touching, like the Samaritan after his golden calf was burned and its remains scattered. No women and no men. You began to be frightened of everything, even inanimate objects, and every human being or animal that breathed, or any bushy tree with sap in it. You thought the trees were ghosts flying at night like owls or crows and you were terrified they might grab you. Your mind wandered, your body was frail, you lost your reason, your smile had gone, and the sounds of the night were tears and wailing. Your mother's heart almost split in half and she almost gave up the ghost in grief for you. Your family failed to convince you that all the things you saw and heard were delusions. They asked each other, "Is this madness, or is it death, or is he possessed?" The djinn. The demon. . . The future became an illusion and the past became a frightening ghoul that was present in every moment of madness. It was impossible for you to get back to normal. There you were living with Frida and Rebecca, Edna and Mark, Siham and the woman with the black dress, Simone, the Romanians, the Moroccans, the Algerians, and the rain, the alcohol, the mud, the tar and feathers, the church towers, the gates of Trinity College, the phantom, the libraries and the post office, Bewley's coffee shop, the Liffey, and the rats and drowning in the land of rain. Specters and ghosts live on the ceiling of the room and hang on to the bedposts. You cry and whimper and scream. You're frightened of the light; you're frightened of the stars. The letters get bigger; the meaning breaks down and you create illusions inside yourself. You feel you are falling down a deep well and the birds are snatching you, and that you're imprisoned in a snake pit and that snakes were wrapping themselves around your neck and the rest of your body. You're frightened of your father and the way he moves around at night. You see him as old and frightening and you tremble at his dull eyes. You scream and keep out of people's sight and you can't face anyone. You're frightened of the smell of people and their sweat and the touch of their hands. You ran away from them, from the sympathetic looks and from their fear of you. You don't want to go to a psychiatrist. Your brother brings the psychiatrist and you run away from him. Your brother cries and says that you are the family's sun and its future, so don't let them down by going astray, and he says that life is good. The psychiatrist gives you tranquilizers: Prozac, Xanax, Zyprexa. You shiver and lose consciousness. Your pulse increases and your heart races. You wander off into the Kingdom of the Lord where no harm can come to you. You have a fit of rage, so your father slaps you on the cheek and hits you with his walking stick. You rave and scream, so your mother takes you to the bathroom and pours cold water on your head and body on January nights. When you don't calm down, she hits you with a stick. You faint and collapse on the bathroom floor and all your body fluids spill out of you. When day comes you crawl toward the closet to hide among the clothes. In the evening, when the demons attack you and your head boils and the faces get darker, you can't stand your body, so you strip off your clothes and you want to run naked toward the flood control channel to throw yourself in. Your sister and her daughter hurry to hide your private parts with their headscarves. On cold winter nights, you run down Digla Street in Maadi, your long hair and your beard reaching your chest. You look into the eyes of cats and dogs and they're frightened of you. You run away from them and fall to the ground. You're almost crushed by the wheels of the cars. You stand in Street 250 for many hours, afraid to move or go back home. Your sister's daughter comes, takes you by the hand, and takes you home to sleep for many days, you don't know how long.

Your niece stayed by your side for many months and missed school because of your breakdown and dementia. She cried when they hit you to bring you to your senses and said, "You shouldn't do that." She defended you with all her strength and said, "He's just a little ill." She patted you, wiped away your tears, and put her tender hands flat on your back, and you could feel the warmth and the calm. She had all the compassion in the world and the mercy of mothers. When you thanked her with tearful eyes, she said, "Didn't you give me a hug after my father left me and went off with another woman? . . . Didn't you nurse me when I was young? Didn't you teach me how to read and how to live? Didn't you bring me story books and tell me lots of stories?" So you give her a big hug and she rocks you . . . as you used to do with her when she was in a cradle, and she sings to you:

One, two, sirgi margi,
Are you the doctor or the nurse?
I'm the doctor at the health center,
I give the sick woman an injection
I give the poor woman a bite to eat
I want to visit you, prophet,
You whose country is far away.

Everyone laments the state you are in. The sheikh comes to recite Qur'anic excerpts over you, such as *By the star when it sets* or *As those who have been possessed by Satan behave*, but that last one may not be appropriate because you haven't practiced usury or dissembled. You've merely fallen in love. The sheikh says, "He's possessed and a victim of the evil eye. The room should be perfumed with the smoke of the incense your brother brought you from that apothecary next to the sanctuary in Mecca, and you should be given the lotus honey that they brought you from the holy mountains of Yemen." He asks you to read verses of the Qur'an as you drink it because you're vomiting it up, because he knows that your spirit has gone astray and isn't around. Then the priest and the sacristan come and wash you with water and holy oil and recite part of the New Testament to drive off the Evil One and save you from your ordeal. And your centenarian aunt comes and chants magical spells over you and mumbles as she strokes your hair with her warm hands and looks at your mother, who is weeping blood over you: the mischievous one has entered the poor woman's house, she has caused chaos, uprooted the plants, and sent people to their graves.

You asked her, "Where are you going, you insolent woman with the evil glint in your eye?"

She said, "I'm going to get all those little babies who creep and crawl and don't yet know their mother from their father."

You pause and yawn, then say, "I swear I'm a victim of the evil eye. Some woman has looked at me," and she says, "He's the best among them," then she finishes off her incantation to ward off the evil eye without looking at anyone.

You said to her:

"I swear to you by the covenant of God, and even a traitor doesn't betray God.

Do not harm him in his swaddling clothes, no milk in the breasts, no horseman on his journey.

The woman's eye has a sharp thorn

The man's eye has scythes

The girl's eye has henbane."

Then she wets her fingers, wipes your brow with them, and spits to her left as she says the words "I take refuge with God from damned Satan and from accursed Iblis."

The images keep coming one after another, and you scream out loud incessantly, and your mind swirls with images of the past, the present, and the future. All that melts away in a moment, and you fly far off toward the clouds that may one day fall on the land of rain.

Chapter 45

One hundred and eighty days later

Hagga Fawziya died: the woman next door and your mother's friend, who used to make you mushroom soup, and who never upset your mother by asking her why you were so reclusive and introverted even when she could hear you screaming at night. She never intruded on you by day by asking why you were so disturbed. She died after a long struggle with kidney failure. You used to see her going out to have dialysis and you were amazed how she could sustain her optimism despite the pain and the fact that her end was nigh. You saw her dying and you caught sight of her stretched out on the ground in front of your house, motionless, her body shrouded, her eyes roaming. The ambulance came to take her away. You suddenly remembered her when you saw the mulberry tree she had planted outside your house. She had asked you to recite the Fatiha for her soul whenever you saw the tree. So death was very close and a fact, but life lay ahead of you, so you were alive.

You stand by the window, resting your forehead against the metal window frame. It feels cold when it touches your skin. Outside there is the flood control channel and the towers of Tora prison, where you can see the outlines of the guards in the distance, and the pale, stunted olive trees on the prison farm. You spot the mounted horsemen on patrol there, you hear the blast of the trumpet, and you tremble. Not far off lies the cemetery, which includes graves for the prisoners. Every morning and evening you see gatherings carrying the coffins of women, men, or children, with bereaved women dressed in black and men with bowed heads. Sometimes the coffin takes its time, and sometimes it flies to its final resting place. Here death comes every day. In the street, the concierge and his wife sit chatting. You're frightened of their looks; you move back a little and shake your head right and left. You rub your fingers and move your feet nervously from the effects of the tranquilizer. You notice that the buds on the mulberry tree have grown in the past months. It hadn't had leaves because the winter had killed off its raiment. You are rather pleased because you've been following the growth of the leaves in recent days, and you saw it as a good omen. "Spring has come," you say. "Perhaps another life will start, with a new beginning." You lean out a little to see the whole tree. You hear your mother's voice calling you, saying she would be happy if you two could go out together, because the weather that day was clear and sunny, and the world was full of warmth. You could go to the Berber Quarter, to Jews' Lane in Moski, or to Mohandiseen because she wants to buy a new chandelier. She's fed up with the cheap, feeble lamp that she has, and they would be doing a favor by buying from your friend who specializes in selling knick-knacks and chandeliers. You do in fact remember him as a pleasant and decent young man, so you say, "Why not?" She helps you get dressed. When she sees you smiling, she asks, "Wouldn't it be better if you had a shave so that people could see your handsome face and your wonderful smile?" After some hesitation you agree. Then she combs your hair for you as she used to do when you were a little boy, and you put gel on your hair and you really do look good in the mirror. You see your face. You look like the child who fell out of the window of your house when young and was saved, and the image of your brother Hussein disappears completely. You go out together and head to the street. She holds your hand as you walk with her, slowly and deliberately.

Now you'd broken completely free of Siham, or so you think. You're living with another woman after returning from Dublin, but you can't hide your love and your old passion for Siham, the paradigm and the dream. Hanan, the woman you intend to link up with so that she can get you out of loneliness and madness, says that you still love Siham. She realized that because you spoke about her so often and wrote about her in your new novel, in order to purge yourself of her. Once you called her Siham and she reminded you that her name was really Hanan, and she said,

"You'll get used to my name when you fall in love with me, and when you fall in love with me, you'll forget Siham, and my name will be your world."

She is trying her hardest to make you sense this love, but there you are, refusing to let another woman take Siham's place, even at moments when you're completely intimate with her. You feel that there's a divide. She has felt that too, but you said it was an existential feeling that has been with you since you were an only child, that you don't reach the point of dissolving or merging with the Other. Then, when you grew up, you philosophized your feeling, saying it was the alienation that the philosopher Albert Camus spoke about, that is the nihilism of existence and of human suffering, and sometimes you cite the Quranic theory that man is created alone and will also die alone.

Hanan says, "God created Eve to kill this feeling inside Adam but Adam didn't want to forget. He wanted to enjoy paradise on his own and he always accused Eve of causing the Fall, which led to Hell, though she was content to be with him anywhere regardless. What matters is that they were together."

She is always with Moataz. Now she goes downtown with him, to attend literary seminars together, and she encourages him to read his stories to the audience. She takes an interest in the covers of his novels, choosing the most suitable ones, and gives him the books he wants to read but is too thrifty to buy. She picks his ties, helps him choose his clothes, and asks him to dress as smartly, as they say he used to dress. She asks him to let his hair grow a little, to lose weight so that he can move more easily and be more optimistic. She told him that her life had started with him and that she would be content with little from him in the way of material support and love. She said that she would help him find his heart's desire and if he couldn't do so alone, then she would try with him, and that she would give him plenty of space to move about so that he could gain experiences for writing and creativity, and that she would produce for him a child that would inherit his beautiful mind. She said she would compensate him for the years of deprivation and wandering. She asked him to touch her hair and her hand so that he could feel her and her presence, so that he would know that she was real and not an illusion. She asked him to let her spirit come into his force field, so that harmony would come about. Even if he didn't do that, she would wait and wait till the end to win from him the love she wanted. Then she said she would do everything possible to make him comfortable. She would ask her father to let her have her inheritance in advance to help him live a decent life. If he wanted, she would open a private publishing house to publish his books, which the government hid away in warehouses and prevented from reaching readers. She said that she also dreamed of building a country house on Lake Qarun, their favorite place to live together. He could write too, and if she got some money she would try hard to buy him an apartment in Alexandria overlooking the sea in the Mahattat al-Raml area, which he loved, so that he could wake up with the sea outside and feel optimistic and write.

They would walk along the seafront and the waves would take them by surprise by hurtling toward them, spraying them with foam and mist on cold February nights. This would be a beautiful scene: the waves striking, gently and with force, against the rocks on the shore like a man and a woman in the act of making love and at the moment of release, and she would escape toward his chest for him to hide her in his arms. She would wipe the water from his face, and he would dry her hair with his fingers and hug her, and the clean, moist sea air would refresh them, and they wouldn't care about the water that flooded the pavements and soaked their shoes, and they would find two seashells and whisper their wishes into them. The wish she whispers would be to stay with him forever, and he would pray that with her he would produce a boy as good-looking as her. Then they would throw the two shells into the sea, and look together toward the castle lit up there, and she would hold his hands and kiss the palms gently and he would look at her tenderly and kiss her brow quickly, and she would notice that he was looking at the distant firmament, the lights of which were glittering in the darkness, and the passers-by, the lovers, and young people would smile at them, and perhaps the lovelorn would ogle them on the sly.

Then they cross the road along the shore and are taken by surprise by the wind. The tail of her coat goes flying and she catches it with her hand. He throws his woolen scarf around her neck, and she feels as if he is her father and her lover. He'll take her out to dinner at the Elite or the Alexander, and they'll have their dessert at Délices and listen to the music. And she'll take him to dance in the Athineos bar. They'll stay a night in the Hotel Crillon and another night in the Semiramis, and their room will be right on the sea. He will live and he will love her more, although she very much doubts that will happen because he runs away from her physically and emotionally. But, with tears in her eyes, she says she will not despair, because she is his beloved and if he wanted she would play the role of lover too, and she wouldn't mind acting as his mother, whom he loves very much, if that's what he wants. With time he'll improve. He'll be the most beautiful lover, the most faithful friend, and the kindest of men.

The water cannon and the policemen's machine guns were aimed toward the protesters of the Kefaya and March 6 movements. Abdel Basset Hamouda's song "I don't recognize myself" was drowning out the sound of Abdel Wahhab's "Gondola" and the jingles of FM Songs radio.

You stood stunned by what was happening. Things had changed and people were no longer as placid as the Nile. Ocean waves were sweeping Egyptians away. Some of them were demanding change, others were demanding a new presidency, others an economic recovery, others the evacuation of coalition forces from Iraq, or a homeland for the Palestinians and an end to Israeli settlement building on their land. The demands were intertwined as security forces clashed with unarmed protesters, and the police showed their strength and might with full proficiency and dedication.

209

Moataz joined the crowds, chanting with them, impervious to the police batons. He felt that he had recovered his senses, but he was weeping bitterly over what had passed.

If you saw him now, he would look completely different. He might be driving a late-model car, with his wife and son sitting beside him. They go into Madbouly's bookshop, then cross the street to Groppi's. On both sides of the street there are election posters for the next president: pictures of Gamal Mubarak, Ayman Nour, ElBaradei, Omar Suleiman, and Osama al-Ghazali Harb, and pictures of men and women he had never heard of, except for one picture of someone he missed and would always miss because he was like a father to him. Moataz would meet you and laugh or maybe frown at you, but it wouldn't matter. What mattered was seeing him, and being happy that he was still present among you, even if he wasn't exactly the person who had gone abroad and come back.

An ending that could possibly be a beginning.

Glossary

Abdel Halim Hafez: An Egyptian popular singer active in the 1960s and 1970s

Abu Nuwas: One of the greatest classical Arabic poets (d. 814 CE), best known for his poems on wine, revelry, and homoerotic themes.

Aqsa Martyrs Brigade: A Palestinian militant group active in the West Bank and associated with the Fatah movement.

Charles Stuart Parnell: The most prominent Irish nationalist politician of the late-nineteenth century.

Djinni (Genie): A supernatural creature in Islamic theology and Arab folklore. The plural is djinn.

Fatiha: The first chapter of the Qur'an, known by heart by most Muslims and recited on many occasions.

Good Friday Agreement: The 1998 agreement between the British government, the Irish government, and political parties in Northern Ireland. It paved the way for peace in Northern Ireland and a power-sharing agreement in the British province.

Kamal Abdel Gawad: One of the main characters in Naguib Mahfouz's *The Cairo Trilogy*.

Kefaya: A protest movement launched in 2004 in opposition to the idea of Egyptian President Hosni Mubarak's son inheriting the presidency. It contributed to the atmosphere that led to the revolution of 2011.

Mashrabiya: Intricate wooden lattice work used mainly in traditional windows in Arab cities.

Michael Collins: An Irish nationalist leader who fought British rule in the early twentieth century.

Mustafa Kamel: An Egyptian nationalist lawyer active in the early twentieth century.

Saad Zaghloul: An Egyptian nationalist prominent in the Wafd party; briefly prime minister.

Shubra: A working-class area north of central Cairo.

Tuareg: A Berber people with a traditionally nomadic lifestyle, the principal inhabitants of the Saharan interior of North Africa.

Wafd party: The main Egyptian political party opposed to British rule between the end of the First World War and the overthrow of the monarchy in 1953. It remains active.

Zaqqum tree: In Islamic mythology and in the Qur'an, a tree that grows in Hell.

Modern Arabic Literature

The American University in Cairo Press is the world's leading publisher of Arabic literature in translation.

For a full list of available titles, please go to:

mal.aucpress.com